The 'H' Letter

The 'H' Letter

Alan Bartlett

Ashford Press Publishing
Southampton
1988

Published by Ashford Press Publishing 1988
1 Church Road
Shedfield
Hampshire SO3 2HW

British Library Cataloguing in Publication Data
Bartlett, Alan
The 'H' Letter
I. Title
823'.914 [F]

ISBN 1 85253 065 0

Printed and bound in Great Britain at
The University Printing House, Oxford.

Contents

Introduction

A popular children's pastime is to connect a series of numbered dots together and in so doing to transform a mess of printer's ink into an easily recognised picture. The framework of this book is a sequence of events which directly resolve a puzzle which appeared to surface in 1941. It also provides an explanation to that which has baffled many peope for many centuries.

On 30th January 1933 Hindenburg appointed Hitler as Chancellor of Germany. In June 1934 Hitler, Hess and Goering devised Operation Reform, which led to the execution of Roehm by Himler and Heydrich. On 28th March 1938 Hitler, Ribbentrop and Hess instructed Henlein to prepare for Operation Green for the attack upon Czechoslovakia. In August 1940 Hitler, together with his general staff, began to plan an attack on Russia scheduled for autumn 1940, and named it Operation Barbarossa. It was afterwards deferred until spring 1941. Molotov had confirmed to the Germans that the Russians' main interest in Europe was complete control of the Baltic and Black seas. In November 1940 Hitler issued his first directive on Operation Barbarossa confirming that the attack would be mounted in the spring or early summer of 1941.

On 10th May 1941 Hess, the Deputy Führer, arrived in Scotland. He had flown from Ausburg and used a parachute as a means of descent. He had been interviewed by the Duke of Hamilton. On 13th May 1941 Winston Churchill issued instructions as to Hess's treatment. He was allowed no contacts other than those determined by the Foreign Office. He would be secured by special guardians, initially housed in the Tower of London and then confined to various safe houses, the first being at Aldershot. On 12th May 1941 Hess was interviewed, denying rumours that any attack on Russia was being planned. He was again interviewed on 14th May 1941. He added little to his previous statements. On 15th May Hess was again examined, the only additional information being an explanation for his desire to meet with the Duke of Hamilton. On 10th June Hess was finally interviewed by Lord Simon on behalf of the British Cabinet. On 22nd June 1941 Hitler implemented Operation Barbarossa and attacked Russia.

On 6th October 1945 Hess was deposited in Nürnberg for trial, and thereafter incarcerated in Spandau prison. He died there in 1987.

But this is more than a child's puzzle. It has dimensions of time and space.

Hitler's knowledge of British history was as comprehensive as that of an Englishman's understanding of Austrian history, virtually confined to prejudiced assessments of epochs wherein the paths of each country crossed. But the Führer enjoyed one advantage. He had learnt of the machinations of European aristocracy during the nineteenth century, their intentions and the consequences of their ambitions which were ultimately destroyed by the 1914–18 Great War. That section of European society apparently embraced its counterpart in the United Kingdom and indeed dominated it. As far as Europeans were concerned, the British Empire was but one jewel in the crowned heads' secret society. The focal point and therefore the first dot in this dimension is the tiny duchy of Saxe-Coburg-Gotha headed by King Leopold of the Belgians, known as the "Mentor of Europe", the "Nestor of Sovereigns" and, to himself, the "Atlas". There were grounds for such descriptions.

The numbered dots continue with the second marriage of Princess Victoria Mary Louisa, Princess of Leiningen, on 11th July 1818 to Prince Edward, Duke of Kent, whose only daughter, Alexandrina Victoria, became Queen of Great Britain and Ireland and Empress of India. Thus Queen Victoria was the daughter of a princess of Coburg. Her Consort, Albert, was the son of a reigning duke of Coburg. The Mentor of Europe had spread his tentacles into Austria, Britain, Russia, France, a vast number of mid-European states and even Mexico. Little wonder that with the background knowledge of the evolution of Europe and the impact and influence of such families as the Hapsburgs, Brandenburgs, Hindenburgs, Hohenzollerns and Coburgs, Hitler should assume the continuity of that influence through covert communication across societies still dominated by class. He feared the power based upon wealth of the Jews. He was impressed by the influence of the so-called ruling classes which relied upon land as their source of strength. So he attempted to destroy the first, but allowed the second to survive to be used as and when he needed. He was wrong on both counts. The Jews he could not destroy. The ruling classes had far deeper roots than the transient tentacles of families flush with ambition but devoid of assets.

So we arrive at the third dimension of the game which starts from a dot at the 15th June 1215 when in England its Barons obtained the assurance of maintenance of ancient custom and law and invoked a system of control of power known as the Articles of the Barons. They became the keepers of the nation's conscience and the King was no longer above the law.

It is not only the passage of time which obscures these dots in the overall pattern. The essence of continuity is that even the most significant steps are achieved without public acclaim and distortion. Historians can provide us with many dates of important events but it is the lines rather than these discrete dots that dominate the solution of the labyrinth. They are synonymous with the Percys, the Hotspurs, the Beauforts, the Staffords, the Fitzgeralds, the Howards, the Dudleys, the Salisburys and the Talbots, and all those quiet dynasties whose devices formed a shield supporting a monarchy contained by feudalism.

The gap in the lines and the absence of significant dots occur betwen 1850 and 1914. That period coincides with the incursion of European patronage into the citadel of English aristocracy.

But what is the picture that actually emerges as the drawing is completed? What is the significance of the following facts:

1 Hess had been involved personally from the very beginning in planning Operation Barbarossa and in masterminding the intended attack upon Russia, both as to timing and method. If he did not comment upon it, why not? If he did, to whom? Why was he not interviewed immediately on his arrival by Churchill himself? Is it conceivable that Hitler would not have taken a personal interest had such an opportunity presented itself to him?
2 How could Hess, at best an inexperienced pilot, fly at night with no navigation aids across a war-torn Europe sensitive to any unidentified intruder; locate a precise position in eastern Scotland, meet a member of the aristocracy, all without very considerable assistance in every sense?
3 Why was he isolated from general interrogation until after Operation Barbarossa had been released? Why was he continuously incarcerated at the insistence of the British, who

chose to blame the Russians? Why did Stalin only believe what Churchill assured him to be true, on the basis that Churchill must himself be ignorant?

The beauty of hindsight is that it enables us to relate discrete pieces of knowledge and discover that which was hidden from the general populace but well known to a select few at the time. It does not guarantee total understanding but it does facilitate a sensible comprehension. Perhaps it also helps us to appreciate more accurately immediate past and current events so that we are less likely to be misled by those who seek to manipuate power for their own benefit.

Fortunately, the Articles of the Barons endure, and those who inherit its responsibilities constitute an on-going shield which, in the long term, is our protection against the abuse of power. Liberty is not Freedom. Those who enjoy the latter do so within the confine of walls that must be sustained and guarded by men whose vision exceeds the range of those who relax within.

CHAPTER I

Queen of the Cotswolds

THE pock-marked face of the Queen gazed serenely down on her carefully coiffeured courtiers bent on their tasks of exciting the admiration of some and casting fear and trepidation into the hearts of others. The fact that they were immobile did little to erase the impression that they strutted and preened themselves in the slanting rays of the autumnal sun. A faint semblance of a mist gathering in the grounds enhanced the seasonal dimension.

The Queen of the Cotswolds had reigned for centuries. Her human counterpart in London had ascended the throne of England but a few paltry years before that evening in late September 1845. The advantage that Victoria enjoyed in terms of her complexion exemplified that in her England, even disease had been encouraged to recognise the class structure. The chasm between each social segment had been broadened and deepened to such an extent that contagious elements were contained, isolated and eliminated. It was not always necessary to complete the process of disease elimination in the lowest orders as long as the epidemic could be confined.

The ravages in the face of the stone Monarch had been created by earlier dissension. Men had taken advantage to hide within her walls using her as their shield. Others had pursued and attacked them in an attempt to destroy in some instances even their brothers. The attackers had struck her repeatedly with cannonball and bullet but the damage they inflicted was superficial. Her countenance remained perfect in proportion and feature. Serenity continued to reign in that cool and pleasant churchyard set on a high hill. The conflict between the Royalists and the Roundheads was but a chapter in the saga of many centuries past and to come.

The courtiers enjoyed a peculiar history. Try as they might, they could not exceed ninety-nine in number. Even so, their numerical strength was sufficient to achieve their purpose, and as the years passed their monopoly permitted increasing stature, pomp and circumstance. In the event of the death of one of them, succession was certain and maintenance of the magical number assured. Or at least so it was said. Painswick churchyard could never lay claim to one hundred conifers.

Yew trees have two roles to play. Their first is to discourage grazing animals, particularly cattle and sheep. This they achieve by providing an indigestible and generally lethal fodder in the form of their foliage. The sexton had no need to concern himself as to the security of his keep when it was protected by stiff green sentinels whose brown boots were firmly locked between the mounds of grass and stone. Their second task, willingly undertaken, was to enhance the last impossible dream by adding serenity, pleasing form and colour to a resting place for all the empty husks of man, woman and child whose past ambitions were of no interest to their immobile counterparts. It was sufficient for them to prosper and grow, changing raiment regularly, standing straight and aloof, resisting the elements of weather. Pride is not confined just to man and beast.

The lych-gate was, as usual, unlatched and swinging idly in the evening breeze, the tune of its rusty hinges beginning to fade as the mist added moisture to the metal. An intruder paused as he pushed the gate wide enough to allow entry to the churchyard. This he achieved by thrusting out his right knee. He was tall, thin and garbed in black. The weight of the past and the lack of a future had combined to drag his shoulders forward and down. As he stood framed in the black-beamed gateway, he looked for all the world like a solitary crow poised to descend from a lofty height. It was a temporary image, lost in the blink of an observer's eye. The man reverted to his undeniably human form as he strode into the hallowed plot.

It was as if the yew trees had changed their role from courtiers to that of a Guard of Honour. As he walked between them, the man's paces became martial in length and timing. Automatically he squared his shoulders and raised the level of his gaze. In so doing he saw the figure at the end of the line of trees step forward into the centre of the path and begin to match him step for step.

When the men were about a yard apart they stopped, facing each other, making no attempt to shake hands. The outline of the crow was matched by that of the pigeon.

The taller man spoke quietly in brief sentences, giving the impression that he wished to get the business between them over as quickly as possible.

"Stockmar, I presume?"

"Yes, Your Grace."

"This is our first meeting and probably our last. I want you to understand clearly what is in my mind."

"Certainly, Your Grace."

"I am aware of your organisation, your intent and the ambitions of your master. You may safely take it that we shall do our best to thwart both of you."

"I believe you have been badly misadvised, Your Grace."

"I do not think so. I have heard or seen nothing as yet which would persuade me otherwise."

"Then I can only hope that you will have reason to change your opinion as time passes."

The crow ignored the last comment. "Stockmar, you and your master are unwelcome. We are obliged to accept your protégé, but unless or until I am persuaded otherwise, we shall maintain our distance and therefore our independence."

The pigeon almost pouted. "I quite understand, Your Grace – t'was in fact the least that we expected. I hope you will have occasion to change your mind, as I am sure there is one matter in which we all share a common purpose and that is the glorious expansion of your empire."

The crow grunted. "For whose benefit? Which brings us to the reason for this meeting. You know me, and I know you. Whatever our public gestures, I regard you and yours as enemies of the State. For the time being you have us at a disadvantage. I think we will outlast you and therefore I am prepared to wait. But do not be deceived. If your activities become too overt we shall take whatever action is necessary to frustrate them. We put this nation's security above all other matters and there are no lengths to which we would not go if we thought that it was in danger."

"Your Grace, I have not the slightest doubt as to your sincerity of purpose and I shall report accordingly. As far as I am able to judge, I am still firmly of the opinion that we have more common ground between us than disagreement."

"I think not, but we shall see." So saying, the taller man spun on his heel and marched rapidly back the way he had come. His strides were swifter and more resolute than before and his carriage was one of purpose, accelerated by a sense of urgency. The second man stared thoughtfully after the retreating figure. He bit his lower lip and then turned his head to look thoughtfully at his companion, who had remained hidden behind one of the trees. More to himself than to anyone, he said, "We shall have to be very, very careful."

CHAPTER II

Resurrection

TAKING tea is an English habit encircled with ritual but quite untainted by religion. It is a pleasant enough pastime provided that those who participate are suitably endowed by nature with three hands or the professional ability to balance simultaneously incongruous items such as cups, saucers, plates, knives and forks. Breeding is confirmed by acknowledgement that tea always precedes milk. The origin of this little rule was simply that the hostess would pour the tea and the butler would enquire thereafter as to the choice between lemon or lactic fluid. Taking tea became synonymous with vicars and drawing-rooms, the former becoming genetically adroit at consuming all without the slightest suspicion of crumb or spot.

There can be no more delightful experience than the observation of this ritual seated on a chair, with hands relieved by a table of any responsibility other than that for which nature designed them in conveying the inevitable cucumber sandwich from plate to mouth in a typically English location. Yet despite the added luxury of a warm, sunny June afternoon, the three men being served on the bank of the river Thames outside the Compleat Angler at Marlow appeared to be quite oblivious to the pleasure they should have been enjoying.

They had been obliged to suspend their conversation whilst the waiter had poured the tea. That operation completed, he was quickly sent away. Even then they forbore to return to the subject of their conversation until he was well out of earshot. The youngest member of the trio spoke first.

"I have not the slightest doubt but that the original was destroyed. McDonald himself delivered it to my father. The envelope was sealed and had obviously not been tampered with." The speaker paused to brush away a persistent wasp apparently determined to commit suicide in the strawberry jam, giving the senior of his two companions the opportunity to ask:

"Did your father destroy it immediately?"

"Not immediately. He telephoned several people to get their approval for its destruction. I don't know how many. I only know of two for certain but there could have been others."

"Did he read the contents?"

"There was no need. He was made aware of what was in it when he was advised that it was on its way. To the best of my knowledge and belief, the envelope was burnt with the seal unbroken."

"So the existence of the letter was known to a number of people but we do not know how many were aware of its contents. Was it known that it had been destroyed unread?"

"Absolutely. My father insisted on having two witnesses present when he burned the letter and its contents. One was McDonald who originally delivered it and the other was Urquhart, both of whom have since died. My father left no papers or any information regarding this matter. We have gone through all his strong boxes and personal files and have found absolutely nothing."

His inquisitor picked up his cup and saucer and thoughtfully sipped the rapidly cooling tea. "But he told you of the incident?"

"Of course. That's how I know and I am also aware of the implications."

"Quite, but you didn't seek to extend your knowledge by asking questions?"

The other nodded, refraining from commenting on the implied criticism. The third member of the party, who so far had remained silent, added his contribution.

"It appears that we shall have to identify everyone who could have known of the letter and particularly those who were advised that it was en route and therefore might have had some knowledge of its contents. And that is not going to be easy some forty years after the event."

The youngest of the three was quick to grasp the inference of the passage of time. "There's more than an even chance that the great majority of those that did know must now be dead?" His enthusiasm was quickly dampened.

"That is undoubtedly true, but that only makes the task more difficult since there will be fewer leads for us to follow. Even if they were all dead, we could not relax because now we know that someone is alleged to have a copy."

A young couple had taken the table next to the trio and, whilst they were obviously enamoured with each other to the point of complete exclusion of their surroundings, there was an immediate common consent that the conversation should be changed to one of generalities.

"I will give you a ring in about a week's time to see if you have been successful and to arrange further meetings which may be necessary. In the meantime I will make enquiries as to the origin and substance of the claim." The speaker had uncoiled his length during his proclamation, at the end of which with the briefest of nods he turned and walked somewhat stiffly back to the car park. There a liveried chauffeur jumped smartly out of a Rolls Royce to open the passenger door eliminating any impediment to his master's passage.

Of the two remaining at the table, one made his way into the hotel and the other walked slowly towards his car, the design of which had never intended there to be provision for anyone other than an owner driver.

Perhaps it was the isolation on the riverbank or the realisation that there might be time for a pre-dinner tumble or some other external factor, which prompted the courting couple to retire also into the hotel without first having tasted the pleasures of taking tea on an English summer afternoon.

CHAPTER III

London

ONE benefit of long legs is that it is possible to climb stairs quite rapidly and comfortably by taking two steps at a time. The impression is that of mercury defying gravity in its progress from bottom to top. Audley took advantage of his height to flow smoothly yet without apparent haste over the carpeted ascent from reception to first floor in the Carlton. Despite the efficiency of his progress, several dignified eyebrows were raised by descending members from whom age had long since removed any elasticity stretched in their legs. But Audley was late, a fact that he detested and knew that his host would find wholly unacceptable. He therefore ignored convention and accelerated his progress. Upon entry into the bar, he wasted no time on explanation, which in any event would have sounded like an excuse. He could only apologise for a fact. "Sorry I am late, Sir, I hope it did not inconvenience you?"

His host was standing away from the long mahogany counter, immaculately dressed, and holding a tumbler of malt aqua vitae. He looked thoughtfully at Audley. "What will you take?"

"A tomato juice, if I may."

A nod to the ever-waiting steward was the only indication of approval. In fact, Audley's request was absolutely right. He needed a clear head. He would be expected to partake of the club's excellent claret over dinner, and an alcoholic request could have led to a number of faux pas later in the evening. He had recovered some of the ground lost by his late arrival.

"We have a corner table. There is only the two of us, so a room would have attracted attention. How did you get on?"

Audley waited until the steward had completed his cycle of delivery and returned to his post behind the mahogany demarcation. "Not at all well. I have nothing new. There is no doubt that the letter was destroyed, and we still do not know with certainty the identity of all those who knew of its true purpose and contents."

"So what have you done?" The question was quickly asked without any allowance for equivocation.

"Urquhart died some ten years ago. He was a batchelor. McDonald died twenty years ago. His wife died about thirteen years after him and they had one son, who is a chartered accountant in the City. I have arranged to meet him tomorrow. His father may have told him something."

"Good." Audley's host pursed his lips. "But not enough. What else?"

"I believe that the next move should be in Germany. Although we may find some survivors in this country who knew of the letter and its contents, it is extremely unlikely that anyone would have committed anything to writing. I am absolutely certain that no copy or reproduction of the letter or any part of its contents was taken or made in this country. I am as certain about that as the fact that the original was destroyed."

"In short, you are saying that we should now assume that if there are any documents relating to the letter they can only be copies or extracts made or written at the source of the sender, rather than the recipient?"

"Yes Sir."

"Ah, but there is one other possibility. It could have been copied en route."

"Admittedly so, but I believe highly unlikely because it was handed personally by the writer to the courier. We knew his plan before he left, and he arrived precisely at the time and place estimated. The courier has consistently and constantly maintained that he never opened the envelope. He has asserted many times that he was quite unaware of the details of its contents and of the whole purpose of that part of the exercise, except that communication would be entirely between the addressor and the addressee. He handed the envelope to McDonald, who was waiting for him and was the first person he met when he arrived in Scotland.

"McDonald was completely trustworthy and had been a servant and companion of my father's all his life. McDonald never let the envelope out of his sight and never indicated its existence whilst he had it in his possession or at any time thereafter. There may have been a short period of time between McDonald handing the envelope over to my father and its destruction, but that could have only been a matter of hours, and I have not the slightest doubt again that it remained entirely in my father's possession over that period. The standing rules for communication had been observed very strictly. My father was instructed by the then Keeper of the Tube who had followed his standard practice of telling but one person. That person being my father, it was then left to his discretion as to the number of people he, in turn, had to advise and instruct. Since he was obliged to keep that number to a minimum, I doubt whether more than three other persons knew of the letter's existence, and possibly only one was aware of its contents. I would expect my father to have made such an arrangement in case something should happen to him, particularly as nothing could be committed to writing. There could also never be any reference back to the Keeper. My research to date suggests that it is more than likely that the two or three individuals who were originally told have since died. Now we have the interesting fact that the extent of my own knowledge is to the existence of such a letter and even I have no idea as to its contents other than that they would have been extremely damaging had they been published. The last is an assumption in view of all the efforts made to destroy them."

"True, but let's continue over dinner." Audley followed his host to the dining-room, which was sparsely occupied; even so, he had expected some recognition of his distinguished host, but not a single eye was turned in their direction. On the occasion of his previous and only invitation to dine, the room had been filled with famous faces. Audley had the unpleasant feeling that his host had in fact arranged private accommodation by allocating that role for the main chamber! Indeed, the other occupants were seated at about three tables distance from that chosen by his host, in a semi-circular pattern that effectively roped them off from any subsequent arrivals. The arrangement also ensured privacy of conversation. His host looked at him deliberately through the candelabra.

"I have already taken the liberty of ordering for us. Some

smoked salmon, then plain roasted duckling, usual vegetables and a bottle of Club claret."

Audley responded with genuine enthusiasm. "Very nice. That will suit me admirably."

"Good. Now let me fill you in, as it were, so we can decide what you should do next."

Some of the facts which were then relayed to him were already known to Audley through his initial briefing, but others were completely new. The whole made for a fascinating historical analysis.

Information is power, and those who seek to exert absolute authority need to be able to anticipate events. This they can only achieve by amending their decisions through the clandestine knowledge of the intentions of others. So, since the beginning of the struggle of man against man, there had been a need for secrets and the acquisition of the secrets of others. In short, a need for spies.

It also followed that as the earliest ambition of man was to own that which belonged to his neighbour, the gathering of secrets was directly related to open conflict. Thus spies were popularly regarded as an essential military weapon. At the very least, it gave those who carried out its nefarious activities a semblance of status and integrity.

But there were other needs for information that were not directly generated by warfare. These were essentially for political survival. A king had to know who might be a threat to his throne; a leader was concerned with the possibility of a coup from within. Both relied upon the combination of their own intuition and such information as they could gather from the whisperings and observations of others. So there were diplomatic spies whose status came only after the successful conclusion of their mole-like careers or became a façade specifically constructed to aid their true intent.

These two streams of information met only at the source of their direction, and those who fished in each were deliberately kept apart. As the centuries passed, Military Intelligence contrived to attain some degree of respectability in return for some publicity. The achievement of recognition had two results: awareness and with it the possibility of misconception. Military Intelligence became synonymous with spies, and the public lost sight of any alternative category. Which was just what those not directly concerned with warfare or its economic implications desired.

Up to the nineteenth century, the demarcation between Military Intelligence and diplomatic spies had been sharply drawn, although there were inevitable connections. This division was assisted by the class structure of European society. Diplomatic espionage was very much the domain of the aristocracy, although there were members of the upper class who had also made the Army their careers. These forged an unofficial link between the two organisations. Their particular value became apparent when the nation prepared for and entered into war.

The military espionage network played a tactical role. Its limitations were predetermined by political intrigue in which it played no significant part. It therefore followed that the source of ultimate power lay with the diplomatic spy-ring both in terms of information and resources, since by its very nature it already commanded most of the wealth within each nation.

The United Kingdom was no exception. Indeed, the Monarchy had contributed both directly and indirectly to the growth and development of a segregated intelligence system. Ironically, however, despite the most determined efforts of a few Kings and Queens to obtain the ultimate power of dedicated intelligence, that had been quite effectively garnered by a very small number of long-established families. From time to time there had to be self-discipline in restraining the use of power to avoid its loss. Certain Monarchs, and in particular Queen Victoria, had achieved a remarkable independence of the Establishment so that considerable patience had to be exercised by the families at such times before overt roles could be re-assumed. Historically, these lulls were temporary, but they could have represented a complete change of direction for the nation – an unthinkable and most undesirable event – had those holding the power of intelligence demonstrated their strength in confrontation. That, their forebears had learned after signing the Magna Carta.

The old man then moved from his philosophical thesis to one of practical interpretation.

Military Intelligence still played a vital role in the United Kingdom despite the apparent absence of open warfare. It used the cloak of national security to contain or attack those elements which in the opinion of its political masters contributed a danger or potential threat. Since the Prime Minister of the day was solely responsible for the country's Intelligence services, it was assumed that his or her directions governed their operations. But that could be only partly true since inevitably recommendations as to policy and tactics had to emanate from time to time from within the service, whose members could present their case without the need for external confirmation and therefore the avoidance of contradiction. Beyond the control of any Prime Minister was the influence that could be exerted from within and without the service from the established but less formal organisation involved in diplomatic espionage. And that was where Audley came in.

He had been recommended as a suitable candidate for Military Intelligence. He could anticipate an approach from that service within a matter of days. The purpose of the dinner, however, was to suggest he should not only accept that offer but also act as a link between diplomatic and military espionage services, taking his ultimate instructions from a control in the former.

"You would have been invited to join us anyway, but I am obliged to hasten your appointment because of this recent development."

"Was my father with you?"

"Naturally, our two families have served together since Good King Hal became difficult."

"You mean the Reformation?"

"Yes. That period of unpleasantness is a good example of the ultimate effect of a number of crises in our history. That which was promoted achieved exactly the opposite to that which was intended. As the Jews learned centuries ago, there's nothing like oppression and the occasional holocaust to guarantee survival and ultimate prosperity. We, on the other hand, have to guard against the inevitable complacency of position and power, so the dangers of this latest challenge are not inopportune. We are the ultimate custodians of our security and therefore our heritage."

Audley picked up his glass of port and surveyed the room. He was not surprised to find that the eyes of the portraits around the walls were glued to his. It was an uncanny sensation to which he had long ago become accustomed at his home near the Severn. He was, however, somewhat startled to find that the expressions were remarkably similar although the sitters were of different generations and antiquity. There was no glimmer of laughter; their gaze was uniformly unemotional; their undoubted successes had left no triumphal expression. What they had achieved was of no personal significance. In their view they had been groomed for their moments of glory, and the natural succession of events reduced any climax to the level of one more step in the long sequence of a climb. Audley had no alternative, but even had it been presented he would have failed to recognise it.

"I understand, Sir. I am honoured that you should feel I can succeed my father in rather more than title."

"So be it. But you must prepare yourself for some unpleasant facts, some equally unpleasant acts and, above all, a dedication that may conflict with your own views and aspirations but which none the less must be applied. I know that you are on the square but even that has to be subordinated where conflict arises. You will have to accept my word tonight because once committed you will be unable to turn back or deviate."

Audley had not heard so grave a tone even at the most significant of all the ceremonies he had attended whether religious or civil. So much so that for a moment he lost his train of thought as he looked into the dark brown eyes of his instructor. Across his mind flitted terrible scenes of silent torture, silent because he had closed his ears, of death inevitable because he withdrew a helping hand, of deep, deep despair following injustice knowingly applied and the awful containment of a knowledge that shocked but could not be dissipated by passing on to others. The brown eyes reflected comprehension but offered no compassion. There was no need to explain the cost or consequences.

The younger man placed his glass on the table to avoid drawing attention to his shaking hand. The room had suddenly become unbearably hot and remarkably still. He opened his mouth but its dryness caused him to cough. For a moment he was tempted to take up his drink, but quickly realised that if anything his hand was even less steady. He drew his tongue over his top lip, an unpleasant but unavoidable action if he wished to speak clearly. "I take it you will let me know who to contact?"

"Surely. Whilst we most certainly will meet from time to time socially, you may safely take it we shall never refer to this conversation or indeed its subject again. I am personally delighted that even if it is a little premature, you have accepted the invitation. I am sure you will continue the tradition very satisfactorily. Now if you would like to take your leave, I think you will find transport waiting at the main door to take you to your flat."

Audley stood up slowly, a little uncertain as to formality. He half expected a shaking of hands with a wish of "good luck", but that did not follow. The circumstances were hardly commensurate with the assumption of a new job or even a new responsibility. He had received part of his inheritance which in reality was a duty. Luck would play no part in his endeavours.

"Goodbye, Sir," were the only words left for him to say. Any expression of thanks would have been as inappropriate as a handshake.

He turned away from the table and walked deliberately towards the door, struggling to maintain an even step and straight back. As he stretched out his hand to turn the vast brass knob the door was opened miraculously by its liveried keeper, who had been standing outside, just long enough for him to continue unchecked across its threshold. There was no opportunity for anyone on the landing to view the occupants left in the room or even hazard a guess with whom Audley might have been dining.

CHAPTER IV

The Second Recruitment

FAMILIARITY breeds security. To the stranger, the square mile of the City of London is anything but golden. It is either an ant-heap of endless hustle and bustle restrained by dirty rain-blackened buildings or an evening morgue in which the gutter is the only evidence of former human habitation. The City is at all times a desert of anonymity – and that suits some people admirably.

Audley was one of the madding crowd through initially misplaced choice and ultimately lack of alternative commitment. By the time he had decided that the daily task exceeded his daily bread in terms of satisfaction, he had allowed himself to become inextricably attached to the web of commerce. He was held by the sticky mixture of money, status, recognition and routine. It was undoubtedly pleasant to be appreciated and wanted. It was very attractive to be able to stoop from a lofty height and extend a helping hand in return for the body and soul of some aspiring and perspiring provincial entrepreneur. But without doubt it was expensive in terms of unnatural discipline, mental gymnastics and constantly changing patterns of justification. Audley made money, lots of it, but he still questioned his contribution to the creation of real wealth. His job was to capture and enlarge the shadows on the wall projected by the flames of a fire from which he was so remote that he had no appreciation of its elements.

Audley had started his City career as a stockbroker, succeeding his father after a decent pause of three days following the paternal demise. Had that event not occurred, Audley would have had to wait for all of two years, that being the term of apprenticeship insisted upon by the Partnership Deed. Partners who held ambitions to accelerate their family's passage up the pecking order had to marry early, which haste could well prove a substantial sacrifice in vain. So such an enticement was seldom seriously considered. Continuation of the accepted pattern of succession was both comfortable and rewarding. Gambling is never a profitable activity even for stockbrokers. Their wealth was derived from those who did not suffer from such inhibitions and whose excesses provided their agents with a certain margin regardless of the ultimate outcome of their transactions.

He had just started to read his post, having already decided that only idiots remained in London between June and August, when he gladly accepted the interruption of the muted telephone.

"Hello. Yes – 'tis I. Who? Don't know him. Says he knows me? Oh, very well, put him through." Audley stuck the receiver between left ear and shoulder in order to continue sifting through the papers in front of him.

"Who? Clerkenwell? No, never. Could have been. Anyway, let's assume you are right. What can I do for you? Possibly – where?" Audley picked up a pen. At least he had plenty of scrap paper for notes. He wrote down an address.

"25 Grant Street."

"Simmonds & Clarke. Oh – about 6.15 p.m. Yes, tomorrow evening. O.K. Right, see you then. Bye." An involuntary shrug of the shoulder caused temporary havoc as the telephone, released from its precarious position between head and shoulder, crashed onto the desk.

"Damn," said Audley as he replaced the receiver and gathered his papers back into a uniform heap. "Curious, don't remember him at all, but he obviously remembered me. Wonder if I'll be able to recall him when we meet. Wonder what he wants?"

As is inevitably the case, whereas Audley left his office 6 o'clock prompt without fail every day from Monday to Friday inclusive, the following evening was the exception that proved the rule. Preparation for a new issue generated an afternoon session that threatened to extend the day. Audley's mind was not as firmly fixed on the job in hand as it might have been. He was recalling his dinner at the Carlton and remembered with some embarrassment that he had arrived late for such an important event. He glanced casually at his watch to discover that he was likely to be late again. That would make it a second time in a row, which was more than enough to encourage a reputation. Suddenly Audley put the two events together. He had been warned to anticipate an approach.

Perhaps this was it. The sooner he found out the better. He glanced quickly through his papers. He could see no obvious point on which he might be asked to contribute and even if he were, it would be too late to incorporate any further significant changes that day. He retrieved his briefcase, thrust the bundle into it and stood up.

"Right, chaps. Must go. Looks all right to me. If there is anything dramatic I should be home by 8 p.m. Meantime, I have an important meeting just around the corner. See you all tomorrow. 10.30 a.m.?"

The round table virtually filled the room so that Audley's progress around it created a bow wave of chair movement and paper adjustment. The fact that he could take such a peremptory leave did not find favour with those forced by lack of seniority to stay until the bitter end. Add to that number those who could have left had Audley chosen to stay and those who felt that duty required their presence, and the total equalled everyone remaining after Audley had shut the door quietly but firmly on his exit.

There then followed a pause, intended to be pregnant, during which lips were pursed or shoulders shrugged, but which, in fact, demonstrated the frustration of the emasculated. Audley was, after all, the senior partner in all but name, and even the timing of the adoption of that designation was entirely at his discretion.

Taxis hibernate when it rains. The drivers are also somewhat robust if the journey is of uneconomic length. Since the first condition existed and Audley knew that his destination was literally around the corner, the only pause in his progress from office to 25 Grant Street was to collect his umbrella or at least the one that on quick examination appeared to be nearest to that which he remembered leaving in the lobby that morning.

There are some streets in the City of London that might well have justified that description before the Great Fire when such thoroughfares were generally regarded more as open sewers than passage ways for carriage and pedestrian. Grant Street undoubtedly fell into that category, although it was doubtful if that was its original name. Its approach was through a narrow arch, squeezed between two grey stone façades that offered no immediate signs of identification. The anonymity continued around its first corner at which point the street was transformed into a tiny square. A quick glance from under his umbrella caused Audley to pause and reconnoitre. Even allowing for the fact that some London addresses encompass several consecutive numbers, the length of the street and the size of its square could never include twenty-five separate residences. The riddle was soon answered. The square was incomplete. As the street entered on one side, it also exited on the other. An even narrower niche offered the street's continuity. Audley accelerated and entered the gloomy fissure. Number 25 was on the left and was approached by a long flight of stone steps contained within a pair of wrought-iron balustrades. To each side of the heavy door shone a brass plate, etched with the title 'Simmonds and Clarke' and the message 'Financial Public Relations Consultants'. There was no aspect of the description that appealed to Audley despite his sorties with merchant bankers and finance houses generally. The pyramid of services offered in the City reminded him more of the analogy of fleas than that of the edifice of the pharaohs. That his own firm might be regarded by the hoi polloi as akin to a leech had never crossed his mind. Critical appraisal is a luxury seldom self-applied by its author.

Audley responded to the inevitable squark-box and was rewarded with an instant disengagement of the main door lock. Mindful that it was but a passing moment and repetition would be an embarrassing admission of uncertainty, he immediately pushed the door open thereby jamming his open brolly between self and threshold. The umbrella cascaded water across the front of his coat and trousers, concentrating more rain on part of his person than he would have otherwise suffered had he not bothered with its protection in the first place.

The door closed with a loud click behind him. He stood on highly polished wood flooring and paused to examine the large damp patch which had assumed a sporran shape and location. It was very wet. There was no possibility of reducing its visual impact, particularly as the suit he had chosen for the day was a very light grey worsted. Ah well, such is life, he thought and turned to examine the directory on the wall. "Reception. First Floor."

At the end of the hallway was the lift. It was a genuine antique. Wrought-iron gates designed to trap, dislocate and if lucky, guillotine the fingers and thumbs of the unwary intruder. A series of buttons protruding from a black box was duplicated outside and within the lift. The buttons were more helpful to the blind than the sighted. Constant application of forceful digits had long since obliterated the numbers which remained impressed out of sight but in touch on the metal. The Victorians did nothing by half measures. Each button was prepared and presented for one particular use, the identification of one floor only.

Audley cheated. He assumed the lowest button to be the equivalent of the ground floor and pressed the one above it. He was wrong. There was a basement. Consequently, he only induced a clunck and a slight shudder. Throwing caution to the winds, he pressed the next one up. The direction was as anticipated but the mode was not. The lift rose, hesitated, grumbled, stuttered and attempted to assert its independence. Fortunately for Audley, its maximum achievement was to finish some six inches below the level of the floor at which it purported to stop. Since its safety features had long disappeared with the natural erosion of iron against steel, the difference in levels offered no impediment in the opening or closing of the gates. Audley climbed out thankfully, umbrella held at the ready. His nose was remarkably close to the glass panel set in a door. He could just make out the gilded letters PTI, the top and tail of the word beyond the focus of his eyes. A reasonable assumption was that the full spelling indicated "reception", so he pushed the door open and entered.

A young lady was seated at a desk which commanded the room in which he now stood. She looked up casually, started to speak, stopped abruptly and riveted her gaze to Audley's middle section. He had completely forgotten about his wet patch. The girl's frozen attitude was more than a gentle reminder. Sangfroid was highly desirable but action prevailed. Audley suspended his umbrella strategically and took the verbal initiative.

"Mr Clerkenwell, please."

"Oh, yes – er, is he expecting you?"

"Yes, although I am a few minutes late." Audley could not prevent himself. "It's raining."

"So I can see."

The rejoinder, equally automatic, reduced the exchange to its starting point. The only course open to both of them was that Audley should proceed to his intended destination as quickly as possible. The transition was quickly realised. At the behest of the telephone, the young lady preceded Audley through another door at the end of her reception area and then stood aside to allow him to enter. As she made to leave, she quietly asked him, "Shall I look after your umbrella?" Audley clung firmly to his shield and shook his head. "No, thank you." She looked him straight in the eye as she walked past him out of the room.

Standing at the end of a long, narrow table was a thick, fair-haired man with a complete set of sideburns, moustache and beard.

"My name is Clerkenwell. Pleased to meet you, Mr Lonsdale."

Clerkenwell motioned to Audley to sit down. He partially disappeared from sight as he sifted through the contents of a drawer on his side of the table, and then placed the results of his search, a plain manila file, in front of him.

"We have the need of a little formality. Before you can answer certain questions which I will put to you, I will have to provide you with some information which, in common parlance, is related to national security. I must therefore ask for your signature on the papers in this file as a precondition to continuing our discussion. I am sure that I do not have to explain their significance, particularly if we develop a relationship."

Audley nodded. "Understood. I have no intention of becoming an author, either now or later!"

Clerkenwell permitted himself a wry smile. "I think you will find that we have made provision for that possibility. Whilst an Englishman may need time, he gets there eventually albeit sometimes quite painfully."

Audley decided he had little to gain by reading the documentation thrust in front of him. There was no room for negotiation. It was simply a question of all or nothing.

"Right. Let me explain briefly who we are and why we would like you to join us." Clerkenwell leaned back in his chair and gently fingered his beard. Audley decided to note the occasions upon which this mannerism appeared as it might of itself be a useful signal to recognise.

"As you will have gathered, we are intimately concerned with national security. In simple terms, we are the Intelligence Service of Her Majesty's Government. There is no need for you to know the total structure or its ramifications or indeed its methods of operation other than those that might directly concern yourself.

"In addition to our career officers, we have available to us the services of specialists who have their own careers in industry, commerce, politics, etc., and upon whom we call from time to time when we feel that they can be of particular assistance. They are in what we call our function departments, not being part of the line organisation. They have no prospects in the normal sense but are amply rewarded when their services are used and, if they so wish, they can enjoy State recognition in the form of an appropriate honour.

"They conform to our general pattern of discipline and each has a control from whom he receives all his instructions and to whom he must report. Except in the most unusual circumstances, he has no contact with any other specialist but he may from time to time come into contact with line officers. The discipline is strict and each does precisely as he is told with no deviation or question. There may well be occasions when the instructions are unpleasant, mentally or physically painful, and may even impinge on religious beliefs. In short, however, you do as you are told.

"Finally, in theory, you can opt out by resigning. In practice it is only possible by mutual agreement and that opportunity would only occur when all assignments have been satisfactorily completed. That in turn may well be outside your control or influence, but that's just too bad.

"Now I am going to pause at this point, not to give you the opportunity of putting any questions but so that I can instead ask you one. Are you prepared to accept unequivocably what I have just said?"

Audley did not answer immediately. Although he had no option, it being rather like signing the Official Secrets Act and he was already committed elsewhere, he felt obliged to pause before responding.

"I think I can understand the need for the Service and therefore the methods of organisation and control. I am intrigued by the possibility of making a contribution over and above that which is simply economic and to broaden my own experience and understanding."

Audley refrained from following up with comments concerning James Bond, 007, alcohol and women, all of which flooded into his mind and presented a host of intriguing possibilities for facetious remarks. Whilst Clerkenwell undoubtedly had a sense of humour if only to survive, it was most unlikely that he would apply it during the course of such an interview.

"Right" – which appeared to be Clerkenwell's favourite word – "let us turn from the general to the specific. We need your knowledge of Germany and the Germans. Obviously we know your background in very great detail, and if you look under the form you have just signed you will find a fairly full commentary on your life to date."

Audley turned over the top sheets in the file but decided he would be wasting his time if he attempted to read the thick wad of closely typed paper that he had uncovered. Even if his meeting at the Carlton was known, it was hardly likely to be noted in any file made available to him.

"I see no point in refreshing my memory. Let us consider it as read."

Clerkenwell smiled. Most people were intimidated by the prospect of reading someone else's version of their private life. Total recall was extremely rare. The human mind had a tendency to obliterate unpleasant memories, and to rediscover their existence was seldom, if ever, a fruitful exercise.

"You will be attached to MI 11, section 17A. As you will have guessed, I shall be your control and you will receive instructions from and report solely to myself. We have recruited you for a highly secret and extremely sensitive assignment, and you and I will be working much more closely together than is normal. You will understand more fully when I have told you what it is all about.

"In 1941, as you will undoubtedly know, a most peculiar thing happened. Hitler's deputy, one Rudolf Hess, flew to England as a one-man mission, seeking to communicate with those in authority in order to bring about a peaceful end to the war. At least that is what the public story tells.

"In fact it was far more complicated and its repercussions were enormous. In the first instance, it virtually destroyed any possibility of total trust between this country and Russia, as Stalin assumed that where there is smoke there must be fire. He interpreted the act as an intention between the United Kingdom and Germany to unite against the Soviet Union. He decided that Hitler regarded the mineral and oil resources of the U.S.S.R. as far more attractive possessions than a small island off the continent. I believe that Stalin was correct in his assumption, but at the time it would have been regarded as treason even to admit the possibility.

"The apparent alternative was quite straightforward. Either Hess was an idiot, namely insane, or he had been sent as an official representative of the Third Reich. The preferred motivation namely that he acted entirely on his own initiative in order to effect some reconciliation was so far from practicality as to fall into the first category. Unfortunately neither interpretation provided any satisfaction whatsoever.

"The Allies compounded the puzzle by incarcerating Hess and

forbidding any access to him at all for many years, and then only under the closest supervision. It was generally believed that he was drugged. There was also a popular misconception that he was so restrained by the sole veto of the Russians.

"The absurdity of the situation was such as to give rise to many outlandish theories – as, for example, that Hess himself had been killed shortly after his arrival in this country and that the occupant of Spandau was an imposter, virtually a man in an iron mask.

"We have a fairly exhaustive file on the whole episode, but even with the benefit of hindsight, it is still extremely confusing. For no other reason than the absence of any positive information or evidence, it has been allowed to gather dust on a particularly well-guarded shelf. Now, I am afraid, the whole subject has been resurrected and the RIP erased.

"There has been much fluttering in a number of dovecots because a possible missing link has surfaced. We have been advised by German Military Intelligence that there is a woman in East Berlin who purports to have a copy of a document that will answer the riddle. And this is where you come in. We want you to establish whether she is telling the truth, and if she is, to ascertain the contents of the document. The only way you can do this is under the auspices of the West Germans, and that has been arranged. We dare not send one of our line men as it is important that whoever undertakes this task is completely unknown to any of the professionals on any side, left, right or centre. In that regard you will be absolutely virgin. At the same time he has to have certain qualities – otherwise he will find the task impossible – and hopefully these you possess.

"Now, I cannot pretend that it is entirely without danger, as nothing in this type of business ever is. If you do precisely as you are told, however, you should come to no harm. I hope you will accept from me that it is an assignment of the greatest national security and if you are successful the rewards will be commensurate. Now that's as good an opening as I need to come to the question of filthy lucre.

"Here is a further piece of paper for you to sign, but this time I want you to read it. It includes some fairly morbid stuff with regard to next of kin and similar matters. But also it includes the recommended annual retainer which you will receive whether you are working for us or not. Whilst you are on assignment, you will of course be reimbursed any expenses incurred provided that I think they are reasonable."

Audley leaned forward in order to pick up the piece of paper offered to him. There was actually nothing in it to occasion any surprise except for the last paragraph. This included the financial terms.

He looked up at Clerkenwell. "That's quite a large sum for an annual retainer. I presume because the method of payment is that you will deposit the money in a Swiss bank account to a number known only to me, that the Treasury will not take an interest in it for the purposes of tax, etc?"

"Besides the natural effect of diminution, we certainly would not want any other department within Her Majesty's Government put on notice as to your exceptional source of income. The primary purpose is not so much avoidance of tax as avoidance of embarrassing questions.

"Now if you will sign it, we can get down to the precise arrangements."

CHAPTER V

The Copy

OH, what a grey day! Even the windows preferred to reflect the light from within rather than allow the visitor to view the outside through their rain-spattered glass. Audley gave up the unequal struggle and turned away in anticipation of his next decision – to bathe or watch television.

The room was well furnished as befits a Steigenberger hotel in one of the major cities in Europe. The bathroom was en suite, less comfortable than one might expect, but Germans and Austrians still clung to cleanliness as an expression of expiation rather than an exercise in relaxation. Measuring up the angles visually, Audley rapidly arrived at a conclusion. It was an 'either or' choice, as there was no way that he could see the television screen from within the bathroom. The decision was made for him. The telcphone shrilled for attention.

"Hello, yes I am he." The conversation was obviously in English. "Yes, Herr Dietz, I was waiting for your call. Where can we meet? Hotel Schwille. No, I do not know it, but no problem. Right – I'll meet you in its café at 6 p.m. How will I know you? Corner table – black moustache – reading a newspaper – should be enough. Right, see you at 6 p.m. at the Hotel Schwille." As he replaced the receiver, Audley mused out loud. What a name for a hotel and café!

The rain had had no intention of changing its incessant attempt to reduce everyone and everything to one sodden level of gloom. Despite its reflective effect on road and pavement as lights were switched on, the contrast between pools of darkness and multi-coloured glitter of neon and headlamp was heavily weighted in favour of the first.

Audley paid off his taxi-driver, careless of the fact that he had over-tipped, "Herzlichen Dank!", in his desire to move quickly across the streaming pavement into the welcome of the hotel. Top coat deposited with the attendant, he found his way to the large café-konditorei, which considering the encouragement exerted by the weather was curiously empty. Audley had therefore little difficulty in identifying Herr Dietz, who seemed to recognise him also. Their handshake was perfunctory, each feeling that their meeting was no more than a means to an end. Herr Dietz gestured to the chair opposite to him.

"What would you take? A brandy and coffee?"

"Just a coffee, please."

"As you will."

The order was quickly taken, during which both men had glanced around to attempt to gauge the possibility of being overheard. Audley had come to the conclusion that that was unlikely since they were surrounded by empty tables. Dietz seemed to have read his mind.

"It would still be better if we talked as quietly as possible; as you know there are devices that can easily pick up conversation many metres away. Now to business. You know that I am a journalist, and I work for the local newspaper which is like your *Guardian* in that it is read throughout Germany. About a month ago I had a telephone call from a woman who said that she had a piece of paper that she was sure would be of interest to me. She was not prepared to discuss it on the telephone, neither could she meet me at my office, but she was certain that I would pay a very large sum of money for it, therefore she had no doubt that a meeting would be mutually profitable. The only fact she would volunteer was that whilst it concerned the Nazis, it was not in any way an exposure of a war criminal – in fact almost the opposite. It was this comment that intrigued me, so I agreed to meet with her. She chose the Konditorei am Goethehaus in the middle of the afternoon."

"What was she like?"

"She was tall, thin, almost white-haired, in her mid-sixties, and gave the impression of being very proud although by no means wealthy."

"Did she give you her name?"

"No, she did not, neither would she give me any address. On the other hand, when I had heard her story I understood why she wished to remain anonymous. Her husband, who had been a professional administrator, had recently died. She had occasion to go through his private papers and by sheer chance had found between the pages of one of his many books a faint carbon copy of a letter which had been carefully preserved. Whilst it was readable, she had come to the conclusion that it was one of a number of copies, rather than the only one.

"The letter was addressed to a leading member of the British aristocracy. It was dated 8th May 1941. The opening sentence identified the courier in whom the writer had complete trust as Rudolf Hess. The signature was that of his leader, Adolf Hitler.

"The woman had no idea how the copy had come into the possession of her husband. She had no doubts as to its authenticity and its potential value. This was enhanced not only by the fact that the letter confirmed that Hess had acted under instruction, but that it contained information concerning British Intelligence which even after the passage of so much time would be exceedingly damaging if published."

Herr Dietz then began to see why he had been approached. The existence of the letter would itself be a scoop of considerable journalistic significance. But if its contents confirmed international doubts as to the credibility and integrity of the British Intelligence services, its worth in the right hands was incalculable. It therefore followed that its possession was extremely hazardous, so that it came as no surprise to learn that the woman had taken the precaution of putting the copy letter in a new hiding place.

"How could such a letter affect the British Intelligence Services?" Audley asked.

"I was being rather precipitate. It appears that amongst other matters the writer identified certain people in high places in the United Kingdom whom he understood were sympathetic towards his objectives. He also named a number of senior Intelligence officers who, he believed, were also K.G.B. agents. The main thrust of the argument was that Britain and Germany should unite to destroy Stalin's power; and the first step, as confirmation of Hitler's genuine intent, was to identify those who might assist and those who might seek to destroy such a partnership."

Audley was at a loss for words. He could only ask: "What arrangements did you make?"

"Since the woman wished to remain completely anonymous, we agreed that she should telephone me two days later at my office to enquire whether we might have a deal. Her price would be D.M. 20,000,000. That evening I met with my editor, Klaus Spuhler, to seek his reaction to the proposition and the potential consequences. He said I should go to the next stage and try to get sight of the letter, but if that was not possible, if I still believed the woman to be genuine, then to go ahead and do a deal with her at the price she sought. He was concerned that if we bargained too long she might go elsewhere in order to start a Dutch auction and in so doing expose herself to the possibility of losing the letter before she had the chance of accepting any offer."

"Did she call you again?"

"Yes, we talked on the telephone and I confirmed that we were very interested. It would not be a question of money but rather confirmation that what she had said was in fact so. I then asked her if she had approached anyone else and she said no and agreed that she would not, at least until after we had met for the second time."

"Then what happened?"

"The second rendezvous was in Berlin. She chose the Plotensee Memorial, which as you may know, is a unique museum dedicated to the resistance to National Socialism. We met by the stone urn which is a memorial to the victims of the concentration camps. She had, in fact, been an inmate of Dachau and was released through the good offices of her husband-to-be. I believe that she is Jewish. Anyway, she let me have some more information which made up the total picture so far as I have told you. We then agreed that it would need an independent third party to hold the cash and the document. We both would have to trust that individual, that he would only release the money when he was satisfied as to the validity of the letter. He had to enjoy the confidence of both parties. The reason why she had asked for the meeting in Berlin was that she was recommending the use of a small firm of lawyers whom she could trust to hold access to the letter.

"The final arrangement agreed was that she would give her lawyers a key to a deposit box. My newspaper would hand over to the lawyers the key to another deposit box which would contain the money. One partner of the firm would examine the contents of one box, and simultaneously another partner in the firm would examine that of the other. They would then meet and, if both were satisfied, exchange keys. Each would accompany his nominated principal and return to the strong-rooms, open the boxes to satisfy their principals as to the contents and then hand over the key. It seemed rather complicated, but subject to confirmation of the acceptability of the firm concerned, it appeared to me to be a workable arrangement. I asked her to 'phone me three days thereafter to give me time to check. Since then we have heard nothing. A week after I met with this woman, my editor decided that he ought to take advice from the appropriate authority, which he did by speaking with the Chairman of the Board. What happened after that I do not know except I was asked to contact you and explain precisely what has happened. I have also been instructed to answer such questions as I can that you may care to put."

"Have you any idea where this lady lives?"

"No, she seemed equally at home in Berlin or here in Frankfurt. We thought about going through the obituaries in both cities at about the time we believed that her husband had died, but other than she said he was an administrator, we had really nothing else to go on. His age now could have been anywhere between seventy and eighty."

"Nevertheless, the only real link we have is the identity of her husband who must have been a pretty influential Nazi to get her out of a concentration camp and in a position to retain an unknown copy of a very, very important letter."

"Ah," said Dietz suddenly. "We might be able to find the records of personnel on the headquarters staff in the month of May 1941 at Reichstag. We might be able to narrow it down to the administrative staff. If that is still a large number we could then compare their names with the obituaries in Berlin and Frankfurt. That might give us the answer."

"Precisely so. There is only one problem – he may have changed his name."

"If he was a high-ranking Nazi that is more than likely. If, on the other hand, he was in the shadows then he could well have survived and prospered without changing his identity."

"Well, let's see how far we can get along that path. I'm afraid there is little I can offer to do which you cannot do better yourself. You know where I am staying. I will wait to hear from you."

By this time Audley's coffee, which he had completely ignored, was stone cold. Dietz made no attempt to reorder and Audley had already mentally prepared himself for reimmersion in the rain. The two men parted with even less ritual than that which accompanied their meeting. They merely exchanged nods of the head.

Unlike London, the rain appeared to spawn taxis in Frankfurt. Audley had no problem in finding a conveyance to take him back to his hotel. During the journey he made up his mind that the following morning he would drop into the offices of Schauenberg who conducted a thriving import/export agency in the Kaiserstrasse and had some very specialised fax equipment which would enable him to take advice.

He was addressing himself to the problem of an evening's occupation as he opened the door into his hotel room, but his thoughts were brought to an abrupt halt by the sight of a large pool of water, the source of which was a very wet black umbrella. He had a visitor who not only had a pass-key but also was unconcerned that he had announced his presence when he could have enjoyed complete surprise. The voice confirmed that its owner was aware both of Audley's entry and his identity.

"Oh, do come in my dear chap. Treat this as if it were your own room."

Clerkenwell extended his right hand but remained seated in the only easy chair. His left hand was occupied holding a cigarette, which Audley found was somewhat surprising as he had assumed that a moustache and beard were more in tune with a pipe than the relatively dangerous and fragile tube of lit paper.

Audley felt unreasonably angry. After all, Clerkenwell was his control and if he saw fit to visit him unannounced in the field, then he had no real grounds for feeling annoyed. Nevertheless, it was a bit much. He had arrived in Frankfurt that day and metaphorically had taken but one pace forward. If Clerkenwell's presence was an indication of the relationship between progress and reporting, then the rein was far too tight for comfort. "I must admit I am surprised to see you so early."

"You mean, of course, early in the assignment? But I am more than happy to delay your news until after we have both had an opportunity of refreshing ourselves." Clerkenwell waved his hand generally in the direction of the mini-bar. After the formal question and answer as to choice, the silence in the room was interrupted only by the routine sounds of preparation, pouring and slow enjoyment of the alcoholic beverage. Clerkenwell had half-emptied his glass before he referred to the object of his visit.

"So, what do we know now?"

Audley had taken the opportunity of putting together in his mind a résumé of what he had been told. There was no point in omitting any material facts as he had no doubt that Dietz had already conveyed all that he knew to his boss, who in turn must have indirectly passed on the same to Clerkenwell. He therefore repeated almost precisely that which he had learned and was pleased to notice the absence of interruption. Indeed, when he had concluded, Clerkenwell merely said: "Which is what we already know."

Audley pretended to be impatient, although the comment was both accurate and anticipated. "So why bother to pursue me so early in the hunt?"

Clerkenwell fingered his beard, dropping his head forward so that he looked at Audley from under his eyebrows.

"In fact, I've come to tell you something. Whilst we have a secure communication base in Frankfurt, what I have to say is best delivered face-to-face."

Audley wondered what was coming next. It would be very easy to underestimate Clerkenwell. One had to keep reminding oneself that he was a professional, a man of some considerable authority in a business which did not suffer fools gladly. So Audley waited.

"I want you to fly to Berlin tomorrow to meet your opposite number. He believes that either the East Germans have been offered the same information as Dietz or the woman is a plant. I had no way of knowing whether he is right on either assumption, but even if he is completely wrong it does mean that our friends are taking a direct interest in this and we are obliged to work with them. Pluzes is a keen chap, used to working at the coal-face with a quick mind and an even quicker hand. We had our suspicions for some time that in fact he was a double agent, and so he proved to be, although the West believe themselves to be his ultimate masters. Personally I would not bet on it. He might even have a third allegiance. The odd thing is that we have had his handwriting analysed and it confirms a psychological assessment that he is not motivated by money. Deep inside therefore he probably nurses a belief that encourages him to take the most enormous risks. His original source was the same as ours so there will be no point in checking out his story. On the other hand, if he provides you with additional information then that will be very interesting."

Clerkenwell pulled a long white envelope from inside his jacket and held it out for Audley to take.

"You will find inside the air tickets, instructions of when and where to meet Pluzes and some additional spending money to avoid any local financial support. I don't want you to use any of our Berlin contacts. Whilst they will have to know that you are there, they will not need to know why."

Audley took the envelope and slid it into his own pocket without troubling to examine its contents. "So this is entirely a matter between you and me, a question of direct instruction and reporting?"

"Absolutely. And to be absolutely secure, I will get in touch with you, but you will make no effort to contact me, except in the most extreme emergency. I have no idea what your programme will be in Berlin. That is entirely a matter for Pluzes. You may be there a few hours, a few days or even a few weeks. Depending upon the duration of your visit, I will arrange our meetings accordingly. There will be no need for you to advise me as to your daily programme as Pluzes will report to his superiors on his itinerary which will also be yours. Any questions?"

"No, that seems perfectly clear, except for one major point."

"And that is?"

"What happens if we find the letter or its contents in some form or other? Would it be all right to share it with Pluzes or leave it with him? Are we going to be partners all the way or have you or Pluzes's superiors a preference?"

"A good point. If something completely unexpected happens, you should know where your priorities lie. If you can acquire the letter or details of its contents without sharing them with Pluzes, that would be ideal. However, that would also be quite unlikely. It is better if Pluzes feels that you will share with him and as a quid pro quo you will expect him to do likewise. Just one word of advice: if you have the slightest doubt whether circumstances or conditions will allow you to keep any information that you have been fortunate to acquire entirely to yourself, I would prefer you to share that information. We must have it, even if it means that it becomes known to German Military Intelligence as well. If they found that you had acquired certain knowledge and intended to keep it to yourself, then I have no doubt we will lose both you and it. We would be somewhat disappointed at your early demise, but have no doubts we would be utterly desolated by the loss of the Holy Grail."

The message was quite clear. The prime objective was knowledge even if it had to be shared. Exclusivity had to be achieved without the slightest risk if it was to be achieved at all.

Clerkenwell made no pretence at looking at his watch. He emptied his glass and having set it down on the side-table, rose swiftly to his feet.

"Once more into the breach. I dislike Germany enough when the sun is shining. Rain makes it even less attractive." Clerkenwell, long in body, short in leg, trotted across the room to collect his umbrella. "Sorry about the pool. They really should have an umbrella-stand. I'll be in touch when you are in Berlin. Cheerio."

Audley automatically replied "Goodbye" as the door closed behind his control. He stared thoughtfully at the empty glass and then said aloud: "I need them both."

CHAPTER VI

German Military Intelligence

Berlin

WOLFGANG PLUZES was short, dark-eyed and serious. A pair of Dumbo-shaped ears supported the remains of a black curly thatch that had long since given best to a thrusting pale forehead intent on reaching his neck, an objective handsomely attained. He was obviously fit, sensitive to his surroundings, giving the impression of a cocked alertness. Had he not been German, his general mien might have attracted a second glance just to confirm he was indeed that which he appeared to be, an ordinary middle-class middle-aged man engaged in the middle strata of his profession.

His English was excellent, not surprising since he had attended an English private school and graduated at Loughborough University.

"Ah, Herr Lonsdale. How do you do? I should ask if you have had a pleasant flight and whether it's your first visit to Berlin, but I am afraid we have little time for small talk. I have my car outside. Will you follow me please?"

Audley was glad he had no baggage. Pluzes set off at a very smart pace, threading his way between the frustrating mixture of hesitant tourists and impatient business people for whom identification of the correct gate was their sole purpose in life, at least at that precise moment. The car was an inevitable Mercedes, low in years and high in mileage. Despite the incessant roar of traffic and the rain-created cacophony of rubber treading water, the noise level within the car allowed normal conversation without any stress of making oneself understood or understanding.

"You will want to know why we are already in a hurry?"

"You've found her."

"How did you know?"

"Didn't, but that can be the only reason."

Pluzes glanced quickly sideways, paused and then seemed satisfied. "Right. We will dash over to C.C. [Audley correctly translated this into Checkpoint Charlie.] The address I have is quite close to die Mauer. We believe that is where she works."

"What does she do?"

"She's an official translator at local government headquarters."

Audley absorbed the answer, thus taking the opportunity of looking at the moving montage of Berlin as they sped towards the Wall. Again the rain interfered with any objective assessment of the city and its inhabitants. As far as he could see, there were no dominating signs of military occupation, and the shops, people and vehicles were unified by comfort and self-achievement.

It had been at least ten years since he had visited Berlin and the improvement was less marked than that which had been visible after the passing of the previous decade. Nevertheless, the advantages of being a Berliner were obviously accumulating.

Checkpoint Charlie had not changed at all. Indeed, except for an improvement in the quality of uniform and a decline in the efficiency of the personnel, the passage of ten years had left no marks. Having cleared the formalities of transit from West to East without pause, Pluzes drove carefully, monitoring each Strasse, following a deliberate path which seemed to meander like the sides of an English field across the countryside. Audley began to wonder whether his companion knew the route and/or destination. Pluzes easily read his thoughts.

"No, not to worry. We shall double back in about five minutes. The conducted tour is essential even though time is of the essence."

"Are we being followed?"

"Unlikely, but we shall soon find out." Pluzes took two right turns in succession, looked in his mirror then accelerated. "Good, we are on our way. We are looking for Wilhelm-Pieck Strasse, Number 110. We are at the moment in the Alexander Platz, so we can't be far away."

Audley felt he could make no contribution to the navigation, so refrained from comment. Pluzes turned the car right and left peering intently through the windscreen.

"Ah, this must be it. Let's see if we can find Frau Fischer."

Pluzes led the way from his car parked at the pavement to a pair of large double doors cemented into the front of a very uninviting block of offices. He pushed at the one to his left and to Audley's surprise, it swung open inwards, a silent invitation to enter. The entrance hall would have deterred the most hardened regular visitor to any D.H.S.S. office in the United Kingdom. The softest of leather-shod feet echoed and re-echoed like those of an oversized Guardsman in the British Museum on Christmas day. A silent traverse of the flag-stoned floor was as difficult to attain as that across the north-east face of Everest. The two men accepted the inevitable and clattered carelessly to the counter.

Pluzes took command. "Is it possible to speak with Frau Fischer?"

"You are?" The question demanded more than a name.

"I am Herr Ebert, a lawyer from West Berlin. I am endeavouring to trace a Frau Fischer who was born Remer in 1924 in Hamburg. She is a beneficiary under the will of an uncle who lived and died in Austria. I believe that the Frau Fischer that works here in your department is one and the same."

"Perhaps so – perhaps not. It is of no consequence because she is no longer working here – and before you ask, I do not know to which department she has been transferred."

"That's a pity because the estate involved is very big and I am sure Frau Fischer would be very grateful to anyone who helped her to enjoy it." The inference was clear. The commissionaire's thick neck that almost hid his collar took on a mauve complexion which contrasted acutely with his pallid face. His voice was quiet.

"Are you suggesting that I might benefit from passing you confidential information?"

Pluzes backed off both physically and figuratively. "Of course not. The thought had not even crossed my mind."

The mauve remained. "I think you ought to meet Herr Zeigner." The commissionaire had pressed a button before he had completed his sentence. It was not a suggestion. There was no alternative. A grey uniformed guard had positioned himself at the main door. Pluzes bowed. "We would be delighted." The response was a sniff, followed by silence.

In the distance, doors could be heard opening and closing. Then miraculously since he arrived silently, a bird-like creature emerged from farthest corner of the hall and twittered across the stone flags. Audley was reminded of an ugly duckling with a beady eye glued to an interesting wriggling worm. Herr Zeigner enhanced the impression by holding his head slightly twisted to one side, using his left eye as the focus setter.

"Yes, what is the problem?" Before the commissionaire could reply, Pluzes had stepped forward and taken over the explanation.

"No problem at all, Herr Zeigner. My name is Ebert" – he then repeated what he had already said, adding only: "Since she works here no longer, I wonder if you could tell me where she lives?"

There was a pause. Herr Zeigner looked from Pluzes to Audley waiting for an introduction then sensing none would be volunteered, turned to the commissionaire. "Is that all?"

"No, Herr Zeigner. He suggested I might benefit if I cooperated with him."

Zeigner twisted his head so that only one eye fixed on Pluzes. "Hmm – that could be very serious. What have you got to say to that?"

"I can understand the misunderstanding." Pluzes hastened to provide his accuser with an alternative to a confrontation. "I merely confirmed that the estate was large and Frau Fischer would undoubtedly be very happy to learn of her good fortune."

Zeigner did not appear to be impressed. He pursed his lips and Audley could imagine his moment of decision whether or not to impale the wriggling worm or let it squirm a little longer. Then, to everyone's surprise, not least the commissionaire's, Herr Zeigner smiled and pulled out a notebook.

"It so happens that I have Frau Fischer's home address here." He tore out a leaf. "Save you writing it down. As far as I recall she has lived there some twenty years so I am quite sure you will find her home when you call."

Pluzes took the piece of paper that had been handed to him and glanced at the writing. "That is not far from here. Well, I am most grateful Herr Zeigner for your help, perhaps one day I may be able to reciprocate."

Herr Zeigner showed his teeth. "I hope that it does not follow that I will enjoy some benefit from the assistance that I have given. I would not wish Frau Fischer to have anything less than that to which she is fully entitled."

Pluzes bowed. "Once again many thanks, Herr Zeigner. I am sure your contribution will not be overlooked." The undertones were beginning to get dangerously near to the surface.

Audley was not at all sorry to find himself back again in Pluzes's car. "I didn't like that one little bit."

Pluzes sat holding the wheel. "Now do we or do we not?"

Audley looked at him. "Go or not go?"

"Precisely. Do we collect £200 as you might say or go to jail. It may well be a trap, clumsily baited and at best it might well be a waste of time. I fear that we are unlikely to see Frau Fischer again. But if we don't go, what do we miss, what will Zeigner assume? But if we do go, what can he gain?"

"That sounds like curiosity and you know what happened to the cat."

Pluzes smiled. "You may well be right, but I think I know why we have had the invitation. We might find what they are looking for."

"And if we do – will they let us come away with it?"

"Only if they don't know that we have it."

"But they may not take the risk and prevent us anyway."

Pluzes started the car. "Of course, you are right. It's quite a gamble, but really we have no alternative. To return now is to give up, which is precisely why Zeigner is relaxed. If we do not accept his challenge, then we will have given up the race and he can continue or not as he wishes. If we accept and we look like winning, he can still snatch the prize."

"So we accept?"

"Of course – no choice. It's just a matter of wits now. First we find the treasure and then we have to find a way of keeping it."

"And finally to survive?"

"Precisely, but I think we can handle Zeigner. If not, then perhaps we don't deserve our present jobs."

As Pluzes had forecast, the journey was quite short. Frau Fischer lived in a flat which was part of a small block in a cul-de-sac off the Prenzlauerallee. The main door was open and the two men walked swiftly up two flights of stairs to find their destination, flat number 24. The name on the door confirmed the identity of its occupant. Pluzes knocked. There was no reply. He knocked again, but this time pushing with his knuckles. Like the street door, there was no resistance. Visitors were obviously expected.

Pluzes led the way into a tiny entrance lobby with the choice of three internal doors. He motioned to Audley to take that on the right while he opened the one to his left. Within five seconds they were back in the lobby together.

"Bedroom," said Pluzes.

"Lounge cum dining-room," announced Audley.

"Then this must be the kitchen and mod. cons." So saying,

Pluzes opened the third door thereby confirming his assumptions. He turned to Audley. "Well?"

"Everything very neat and tidy."

"Yes," replied Pluzes. "A very professional job, almost too professional. No point in going over the ground again. Since we assume we are here because they have so far failed to locate what they are looking for, then either it is in a most unlikely place where a professional would not look or it is not here at all."

Audley added, "They presumably know that it was originally found between the leaves of a book?"

"Naturally, but to address ourselves to the present problem, where would you look?"

Audley did not regard the question as a compliment, rather confirmation that he was the amateur of the two. "Probably only in the obvious places, that is, obvious to you."

"Possibly," rejoined Pluzes, "but specifically where?"

"Anywhere near or on anything connected with writing, including waste-paper box. Between paper linings in drawers, calendars, tubes–" Audley began to see the enormity of the task, but that did not appear to deter Pluzes. "It could be in an envelope and placed under carpets, table mats, within clothes, on a letter-rack . . ."

"Ah," said Pluzes. He walked into the lounge/dining-room. Next to the bookcase, crammed full of hardback editions, stood a small mahogany desk inlaid with pale green leather. He opened a single drawer and surveyed its contents. "She was extraordinarily neat and tidy. Writing pad, envelopes, stamps." He picked up the pad, quickly thumbed through it and replaced it in the drawer. "I think we are wasting our time. Let's go back."

Audley was not inclined to argue. This time he led the way to the door. He half expected to find it barred by some grey-coated giant, so his relief at a smooth passage from flat to pavement was greater than he cared to acknowledge even to himself.

Pluzes remained silent until they had crossed into the West. "There is only one explanation." The statement was delivered with all the fervour of a schoolboy finishing his theorem with Q.E.D. "Frau Fischer did not have the letter on her or in her flat. If the K.G.B. cannot find it after an in-depth search, it is not there. So she hid it elsewhere – but how did it get there?"

"Why wonder how she managed to carry it?"

"Because she was undoubtedly under observation and any unusual act would have been noted. For example, she could not have deposited it in a strong-room or anything similar. She must have followed her normal daily routine with considerable care."

Audley suddenly interrupted. "Suppose she posted a letter?"

"Precisely, that's why I looked at her writing pad but I could find no indentations on the top sheet. Our friends could not have discovered any either, otherwise they would not have allowed us to tread in their footsteps. So if she did post it, it was only with the briefest explanation on some scrap of paper. That would mean that there is only one possible recipient."

Audley felt almost like saying: "It's elementary, my dear Watson"; but reason prevailed. The Teutonic sense of humour might not stretch to Baker Street. Pluzes appeared to assume that Audley must have arrived, somewhat belatedly, at the same conclusion and therefore further comment was unnecessary.

The Mercedes accelerated through the swarm of vehicles vying selfishly and foolishly with each other for precedence at any price. Whether it was the driver's total concentration on the task of relating speed to survival or the radar sensitivity of a city robot, the journey was accomplished without incident, much to Audley's relief. He began to wonder which would get to him first, the mental effort of double-thinking or the physical strain of compressing time and distance into an absolute minimum. He was given no respite even to resolve the theoretical problem.

Pluzes, like most city-based Europeans, lived in a small but comfortable flat which was in the Kanstrasse. The absence of any indication of female occupation suggested that he lived alone. There was, of course, the alternative solution that there could be another occupant of male gender but Audley had a feeling that Pluzes was not a homosexual.

"Would you like coffee?"

The question floated from the tiny kitchen supported by the appetising aroma which always made the drink itself an anticlimax. Audley decided that the comparison ranked with that of the smell and taste of a good cigar. He often thoroughly enjoyed the weed of his neighbour in preference to his own identical tube of tobacco leaves.

"Thank you – much needed and appreciated." A somewhat flowery but genuine response. Pluzes reappeared in the lounge.

"Do make yourself at home, although you will probably have to return shortly to Frankfurt if I am right – or even I am wrong, perhaps!" Whilst he was speaking Pluzes had been glancing through a notebook. Keeping his eyes on the open page, he stretched out his hand first to remove the telephone receiver and then to dial the number he had found.

"Ah, Herr Dietz, if you please." Pluzes then handed the

receiver over to Audley. "He's there – ask him whether he's had any communication from Frau Fischer – don't confine the question just to a letter."

Audley took the 'phone, looking straight into Pluzes's dark blue eyes. The challenge was clear. They needed the truth.

"Oh, Herr Dietz, this is Lonsdale – yes – yes, no I have not met with Frau Fischer. I am having trouble finding her. Can't explain. Have you heard from her since you and I met? Nothing at all, no calls, letters, messages? You are absolutely certain? I see. O.K. I'll be in touch. 'Bye." He replaced the receiver and turned to Pluzes.

"Well, he says not – but I don't believe him."

"Because?"

"Because he knew her name, and at our last meeting he assured me she had not identified herself to him in any respect."

"So you think he has had some contact with her? In which case you had better return to Frankfurt and face him with it. I will follow and we will meet after you have seen Herr Dietz."

Audley looked at his watch, "What about 'plane times?"

"No problem, even if we are unable to fly the most efficient airline in Europe. I'll run you to the airport and you should easily catch one of the late evening flights."

Audley was a little sad at leaving Berlin without refreshing his latent memories of pike soup, Eisbein and those German wines that by coincidence taste the best and travel the worst. But there would be another time. Of that he was sure.

CHAPTER VII

German Intelligence Service Layers

THE reception given to the sharp and bright greeting of the early morning sun in a cloudless sky depends almost entirely on the night before. Except that he had gone to bed rather late and very tired, there had been nothing imbibed or attempted that could cloud Audley's reaction to the welcome contrast between the wet gloom of the day before and the encouraging glare of the start of the new day. As he looked out on the Kaiserplatz, he stretched in every possible direction. If stiffness was the harbinger of middle age, then Audley did his best to eliminate the message. On the other hand, a stretch was as enjoyable as a good scratch. He could now understand the smug self-satisfaction of a cat going through the same exercise in the warmth of the slanting rays.

Audley decided to combine the advantage of his exceptional early rising with the every-day discipline of the German worker who entered his place of work carrying his inevitable briefcase often before his British counterpart had managed to leave his warm bed and stagger with Nelsonian intent and visage to the bathroom. He would go straight to Dietz's office and await his arrival. Perhaps the unexpected reception would unsettle Dietz and encourage an unguarded response.

Audley was only partly correct. Dietz was already seated behind his desk well into his daily workload. Nevertheless, he did express considerable surprise at the identity and timing of his visitor.

As he stood up to shake hands, he remarked: "I certainly didn't expect to see you so early in the morning and so soon after we had spoken on the telephone. I gained the impression that you were in Berlin?"

"I certainly was but I caught a flight back late last night and I wanted to continue our conversation as a matter of some urgency."

"Urgency?" said Dietz thoughtfully. "Why, what has happened now?"

"Nothing has happened as far as I know, but I guess that something has."

"Such as?"

"Frau Fischer has disappeared and I fear probably for good, in the sense that we shall not see her again."

Dietz looked down at his papers which he started to rearrange. "So I gathered. I am very sorry if that proves to be true."

"Why would you be sorry? Because of the loss of the letter or the disappearance of Frau Fischer?"

"Both. The letter would have been a marvellous coup and Frau Fischer seemed a sad and nice lady."

"How many times did you speak with her?"

"As I told you, four times, twice on the telephone and then the two meetings, one in Frankfurt and the other in West Berlin."

"That is all?"

"Yes."

"You are sure?"

"Of course I am."

By this time the exchange had become abrupt and the staccato beat of the words suggested rival machine-guns. The two men had their eyes locked, concentrating exclusively on the accuracy of their words and the interpretation of the responses. Audley decided to straddle his target.

"On which occasion did she tell you her name?"

Dietz paused before replying. A frown crossed his face. "None."

"Then how is it that when we spoke last night, you used her name before I did?"

Audley immediately regretted the length of his question. If he had put it succinctly Dietz would have had less time to think. Dietz, however, was in no mood to be rushed. He placed his finger-tips together, thrust his elbows on the table and supported his chin with the triangle he had formed. His eyes remained linked with Audley's. The reason for his deliberation became quickly apparent. "You are absolutely right. You did not tell me her name, neither did she. I had absorbed it without noticing the source. In fact it was my editor."

Despite the lack of an invitation, Audley felt it would now be appropriate if he seated himself. The conversation had moved from one of confrontation to a mood of mutual thoughtfulness. He decided to take the initiative. "I think we ought to pool our information as there may be hidden relevance to isolated facts when they are pieced with others." Dietz nodded. Audley continued: "There's an obvious connection between Frau Fischer's disappearance and the emergence of the letter. I believe that, although I've no real evidence, she has successfully hidden the letter in that so far, no one has found it. Again based purely on assumption, the one course she could have taken would have been to post it to you if she felt that, for whatever reason, she was going to be prevented from enjoying its publication. She would have had to rely upon you to honour your agreement but she didn't have very much choice as I believe time had run out for her. Hence my question on the telephone as to whether you had had any communication from her."

"As I replied at the time, no, I have not and that is still the case." Dietz paused. "It's a glorious morning and I dislike stale tobacco smoke." So saying he turned and moved towards the window which he opened as wide as the fitment allowed. He beckoned to Audley. "I know it's not a pretty sight, but if you compare the industrial cities of Germany with those of England, one would be very hard put to it today to decide who actually won the Second World War."

Audley stood beside Dietz and dutifully looked at the view. Impressive though it was, it was hardly inspiring. Then very quietly without turning his head, Dietz said: "Two days ago my editor called me to his office and after discussing certain other matters casually asked me if there had been any developments concerning the letter and had I heard from Frau Fischer. I did not find the mention of her name remarkable as I assumed he had been in communication with somebody else who was better advised than I. But it is too much of a coincidence to ignore. He could well have intercepted an enveloped addressed to me with an East Berlin postmark and was just making certain that I was unawarc that it was in transit and that I had received nothing else."

Audley looked at Dietz's profile. "This reminds me of the story of the Dublin city council that decided to declare war on England in the hope that they would be treated similarly on their inevitable defeat."

Dietz smiled. "It is interesting how every European nation has its favourite race or butt for the inevitable jokes concerning stupidity."

Audley laughed. "The English are the world's worst tellers of jokes as they lack the linguistic ability to create credibility."

Dietz had turned away from the window. "I fear Herr Lonsdale that your mission is fruitless. If Frau Fischer has disappeared then the secret of the letter's hiding place has gone with her. And even if it has been discovered, I have no doubt that it will have been handed on to those who would destroy it within seconds of its possession."

Audley understood very clearly. Dietz was advising him that it would be a complete waste of time for either of them to approach the editor since if indeed he had intercepted the letter, he would have passed it on immediately to those who had been manipulating him. There was no way of forcing the editor to say who that might be and even that knowledge would be quite useless as far as the letter's recovery was concerned. Nevertheless, Audley had more than a suspicion that the identity of the party to whom the editor had handed over the letter would be considerably helpful as a final confirmation of destruction or possible re-emergence.

Audley leaned forward. "I wonder if I could have ten minutes with your editor?"

Dietz looked surprised. "Herr Spuhler? I don't think – anyway, he is like God, you have to make an appointment unless he wants to see you, and there is no question of fixing a time or day. His word is your command."

"Well, let's try anyway."

"If you wish." Dietz lifted his telephone and played a short tune with the numbers neatly arranged within the receiver. "Ah, good morning Frau Paechter, I have an Englishman with me, a Herr Lonsdale who would be honoured if he could have ten minutes of Herr Spuhler's time. Yes, I will wait."

He placed his right hand over the receiver. "She is approaching with some trepidation the throne." Both men unconsciously adopted the attitude of retrievers straining to hear their master's commands. After several seconds in this posture, Dietz removed his hand from the receiver signalling the recommencement of the official conversation. His eyebrows lifted. "Thank you Frau Paechter. He will be with you at once." He replaced the telephone and looked quizzically at Audley.

"For whatever reason, you have been granted an immediate audience. By the way, my apologies for talking in German but Frau Paechter confines herself to her native language. Now you will want to know how to get to the sanctum sactorum. Herr Spuhler's office is naturally in the penthouse. You take the main elevator to the sixteenth floor, at which you transfer to the private elevator which you will find opposite your exit waiting for you. That will deposit you in the middle of the sacred plot. Frau Paechter will conduct you into the presence. I have enjoyed our meetings. I am sorry that we didn't bring it off, but, who knows, something may develop again."

Dietz held out his hand. His words were a formality. Yet Audley felt that they had enjoyed a rapport if only through necessity. For whatever reason, he believed he could trust Dietz. "We will keep in touch. If the unexpected happens you can always contact me here." He handed over his firm's card with his left hand as his right grasped that of the journalist. For a moment they looked like the donor and recipient at an award ceremony. Audley half-expected the flash of a camera bulb. Then he remembered the conversation at the open window. Whether or not they were on view or visual record, obviously Dietz was convinced they had been under aural observation.

Frau Paechter was the antithesis of a German private secretary. She was short, dumpy, harassed and anxious. Despite the quality of her clothes and undoubted administrative capabilities, it was difficult to reconcile her appearance with that of the confidante of a very influential executive. She bustled along in front of Audley, taking short uneven steps, covering little ground but expending considerable nervous energy. She clearly regarded speech as an unnecessary mode of communication.

Her boss exceeded expectation. His appearance alone provided conclusive evidence of a just cause for the secretary's anxiety and Dietz's surprise at any variance in his established routine.

Herr Spuhler was the very image of a German aristocrat. Tall, slim, almost completely void of hair on his head, bronzed by sun – both natural and lamp – eyes with unnaturally large pupils with no colour division between them and the white balls framed within ginger eyelashes. Even the scar high on his right cheekbone was reminiscent of the Student Prince image of German university graduates. Audley suppressed a wild desire to greet Herr Spuhler with the phrase "Heil Heidelberg". Yet the editor's smile exuded warmth despite the cold flash of pearly white teeth. The welcome was confirmed by an outstretched hand that sought to endorse his greeting. He ignored Frau Paechter.

"Ah, Herr Lonsdale. A pleasure to meet you. Will you excuse me from offering you coffee but I fear I have to leave shortly for an appointment elsewhere." He motioned Audley to join him on a huge leather settle placed at the farthest point from the mahogany desk that dominated the huge room whose décor could only be described as feudal. The inevitable globe and large marine telescope sought to confirm the international extent of their owner's interests. Two walls covered from floor to ceiling by shelves that just equalled in capacity the space required to house hundreds of handsomely bound books that varied in size from pocket edition to those that demanded two pairs of hands to ensure safe extraction. The third wall was covered with tapestry. Its age obscured its subject matter, which Audley decided was just as well as he sensed that in its original form it might have embarrassed Frau Paechter even to the point of disloyalty. He half-expected the fourth wall to be the repository of a hunter's trophies. He was partially correct in that instead of mounted heads of wild beasts, handsomely framed photographs captured obvious moments of triumph, congratulation and satisfaction. The large pieces of highly polished furniture, whether timber or leather, carefully placed on the gleaming floor between islands of diverse rugs completed the world of one who believed he was the epitomy of a man's man. Whether or not his belief was well founded, Audley felt that Herr Spuhler was formidable and not to be crossed.

"Now tell me what I can do for you." The tone of voice had a hint of impatience and Audley realised that there had been a moment of silence between them whilst his thoughts raced away.

"It was extremely kind of you to see me at such short notice, Herr Spuhler. I will therefore come straight to the point. As you know, I have been trying to find a certain Frau Fischer who alleges that she has a copy of a very important letter which she is prepared to sell. I have been unsuccessful in my attempts to meet her and I now believe that it will be impossible for me to arrange such a meeting. I am still extremely anxious to have sight of the letter, and it is just possible she may have posted it rather than kept it on her person or attempted to hide it. If she did, in fact, do that, she might have addressed it here as the only person to whom she apparently made an approach was Herr Dietz, who, as you know, did meet her. Herr Dietz assures me that he has not received any communication from her and of course I believe him. However, perhaps the letter was addressed elsewhere, or for whatever reason it might now be in other hands. Whatever may have happened to the letter, it would be very helpful if I could at least advise those who employ me whether it is likely that the copy has gone into friendly or unfriendly hands, whether it might re-emerge in the future or whether it has been destroyed?"

Audley paused. Spuhler's expression was no longer encouraging. The German looked at his watch. "It's a great pity I do not have more time to explain but let me say this. One may work for an organisation and therefore have an allegiance to it. But one may have a duty beyond allegiance which may stretch beyond the organisation to whom one owes an allegiance. If that is the case then duty wins and one should take the appropriate steps. This will include the protection of one's duty and that in turn may be achieved by keeping those to whom one owes allegiance in ignorance. I know that you are a very intelligent man and you will therefore understand very well what I am saying. In short, you can return privately satisfied as to the outcome of your mission, with your duty done. Those to whom you owe an allegiance will find you highly discontent with your failure to complete your task. Now you really must excuse me."

Spuhler stood and for the second time smiled as he extended his hand. "You have an expression 'thrown in at the deep end'. To a large extent that is what has happened to you. But I am sure you will swim very well. I am also positive that we shall meet again."

Audley responded making sure this time that his hand firmly engaged that of the German's. His fingers still tingled from the inequality of the first encounter. "Thank you very much indeed for your time and advice. I am most grateful."

Spuhler waved a hand casually dismissing the appreciation. It was a hand that was large, thick and pallid, the appendage of a surgeon who preferred the knife to medicine.

Audley was not surprised to find that he had a visitor awaiting his return at the hotel nor that Pluzes had had the grace to prefer the lobby to the clandestine use of his room.

"Would you take a drink with me in the bar?" The question voiced Pluzes's further preference as to the location for a discussion.

"With pleasure." The two men chose a corner table which was free of immediate neighbours.

"So," said Pluzes. "How did you get on with friend Dietz?"

Audley had had time to consider his response to Pluzes's interest. Even so, he paused before replying.

"As I expected. I believe Dietz is as honest as his profession allows and therefore he avoids as far as he can any deliberate lies. If my assumption is correct, he has had no further communication from Frau Fischer and certainly not had the copy letter."

"So how did he know Frau Fischer's name?"

"His boss had discovered that for him. Apparently he is a very influential man named Spuhler."

"You mean von Spuhler?" Pluzes interrupted. "Yes you are right, he is very influential. Of course, Dietz had already told him of the copy letter because of the money involved."

"Yes, and Spuhler must have made his own enquiries."

"Did you meet him?"

Audley had anticipated the question and had decided to take a chance. It was unlikely that Pluzes would approach Dietz again unless something exceptional happened. Any information he got concerning Spuhler would obviously be third-hand and depend entirely upon how much Spuhler wished Pluzes and his organisation to know.

"No, apparently he is a very busy man and you have to make specific appointments, days if not weeks in advance."

Pluzes's expression did not change as he idly linked together the damp rings on the polished surface of the table with a nicotine-stained forefinger. "So, we have lost our way. Frau Fischer has disappeared and with her the copy letter. We have no idea where to find either assuming either still exists. Difficult."

There was a pause during which Audley ran over in his mind the facts known to him and Pluzes. Suddenly his eyes brightened. "Surely Frau Fischer would have read the copy. She would know its contents. She could reproduce those from memory."

Pluzes smiled. "First," he said, "she is the only proof that such a copy existed and therefore that an original also existed. Without her and in the absence of a copy letter, it is entirely wild speculation. Even if she were free to tell her story, in the absence of the actual document is it likely that she would be believed? And even if some did, could they take advantage of that belief? Secondly, even if it was agreed that a letter had existed, again in the absence of its copy and even in the presence of Frau Fischer, who could confirm that her version of its contents was correct? She might be the subject of manipulation by others who had an axe to grind."

"I accept all that," said Audley, "but if the purpose of acquiring the copy letter is to know its contents, why not extract them from Frau Fischer and then forget about the piece of paper itself?"

Pluzes sighed. "That's the very point. Whilst some would dearly love to know the contents, without evidence to support such knowledge, it cannot be used effectively. As far as others are concerned, the destruction of the copy letter is the absolute defence against exposure. I have no doubt that by now quite a few people have guessed pretty accurately what has been written about what and whom. I am equally sure that the K.G.B. will have successfully persuaded Frau Fischer to recall all she possibly can of what she has read. But all that information based on guess and recall, although interesting and informative, is nothing without proof. And so we are all back to square one."

"Except we know now that a copy existed and might still exist, whereas before Frau Fischer surfaced everyone believed that even if the letter had existed, that it had been destroyed and no copy had been retained."

Pluzes looked into his glass thoughtfully, then held it up to the light over the table. "True, but now we look through a glass darkly." He finished off his drink and placed the empty tumbler firmly back on the table. "Well that I suppose is that. If we should hear anything further of Frau Fischer or the copy letter, we will let you know immediately. Similarly if you hear . . ."

"Surely; sorry I could not be of more help. Who knows, we may meet again. Of course if you are in London . . ."

"Of course, thank you."

The handshake was formal and Audley sensed Pluzes's disappointment which now appeared to extend beyond the assignment and include him.

The German turned up the collar of his raincoat. "You would never guess, but the bright spell has ended. If Manchester is the home of umbrellas, then Frankfurt must be the birth-place of galoshes."

This time Audley had decided to beat Clerkenwell to the punch. He took a taxi from Heathrow direct to 25 Grant Street. In theory the journey did not coincide with the rush hour but in practice any time between seven in the morning and seven in the evening required the patience of the proverbial saint or the capability of a helicopter to make reasonable time into and across London. The travel news on the radio spewed out comments that confirmed the experience and accentuated the frustration of those encased in metal boxes whose wheels were more often superfluous than effective. So Audley's progress, whilst direct in the geographical sense, was anything but when considered in terms of time. Since he did not have a specific appointment, however, he could afford to be philosophical.

The problem he faced was a real one. What and how much to tell Clerkenwell, to whom he owed an allegiance? What to keep to himself and then to whom to report? But the second question would wait. He had to address himself squarely to the first. There appeared to be no option but to tell Clerkenwell all that Clerkenwell himself could have found out from his other sources, otherwise it would be obvious that something was being held back. If necessary he could add assumption, but even that had to be based wholly on the facts reported. The prime factor was that he should assume that that which he had told Pluzes would be known in part or in whole to Clerkenwell. So that would have to be where he would begin and end.

Audley left his suitcase with the young lady at reception. His attire was in its usual immaculate state so her glance was purely casual as she turned to lead him into the inner office.

Clerkenwell remained seated behind his table. "You might have let me know you were coming. I could easily have been out and that would have meant a wasted journey."

Audley sat opposite him. "Well, you are not so I have not."

"Humm. I suppose you want to report. You realise that the procedure is to use the recording facilities elsewhere to save time and provide a permanent record."

"But you are already recording this – so why do it twice?"

Clerkenwell put down his pen and looked directly at Audley. "Right, let's have it then, what happened after I left you in Frankfurt?"

Audley recounted his trip to Berlin, his meeting with Pluzes, his abortive visit to East Berlin and all that which he had told Pluzes on his final day in Frankfurt. Clerkenwell said nothing and made no attempt to write anything down. When Audley had finished, his control leaned back in his chair, fingered his beard and looked at the ceiling.

"Not a wasted journey. At least we now know that the letter existed. We do not need Frau Fischer's corroboration, but we would like to know its contents. As you say, the K.G.B. will have a pretty good idea what was written, but we can expect no help from them other than they may have a go out of spite or possible prevention of repetition." Clerkenwell was obviously thinking aloud, which meant that he had had only some previous knowledge of Audley's activities. His last assumption as to what the K.G.B. might actually do "out of spite" was not at all clear, and Audley decided that he would give that some further thought. Then followed a long silence which was ultimately broken by Clerkenwell continuing his monologue.

"Yes, we must find out what was in the original letter. Good. So that shall be your new assignment. Retrace the events of 1941 and find out who received the original, what happened to it and above all what it contained – and let me know at each step what you find out. I don't want to wait until the end of the trail. Keep me advised at all times of what you have found out, however trivial it may seem. I will keep the dossier here and I want you to retain nothing in writing. We will take a chance that if you are lost, our knowledge will be as up to date as yours."

Audley could not restrain himself. "The implication is that I could follow Frau Fischer?"

"Yep, if you are too clever or too clumsy. You should know that however determined we may be at uncovering the truth, there are others equally determined to keep it buried for ever. And they are pretty powerful."

"As powerful as we are?"

Clerkenwell continued to stare at the ceiling. "In their way, more powerful. Our only edge is that we have nothing to fear from the truth, and that's quite a unique advantage for the Service to have." He smiled and refocused his eyes on Audley. "Right, go to it. Clear your past expenses with Jenny and you can have an allowance for your new job."

He scribbled a few words and figures on the top sheet of a pad of forms. As he tore it off with a flamboyant and quite unnecessary flourish, he ended the conversation.

"Remember, I want to hear from you regularly and promptly. The more I know of what you know, the more likely you are to survive. You might consider it as insurance by double jeopardy. Right, here you are. Good luck."

Audley looked at the form. It had nothing to do with expenses. It was an authorisation to carry a hand gun, with instructions as to training and issue.

Clerkenwell laughed. "Oh – the expenses – I will simply buzz Jenny about them. That's far more important." This was said with a nod towards the slip of paper in Audley's hand: "I've allowed two days at Leatherhead and provision for three-monthly refreshers. Hope you won't need it, but better prepared and dissatisfied than ignorant and dead."

CHAPTER VIII

The Hess File

THERE is only one circumstance where a trail after some forty years lack of use is not completely void of identification. That is when the original journey raised such a stench that even after a lengthy period of time it still leaves a whiff as a marker.

Audley had had the advantage of inside knowledge concerning one aspect of Hess's flight but he was no more conversant with all the circumstances than most Englishmen who had had to rely upon the public information which had been circulated at the time and the assumptions made in various publications after the event. The whole escapade was so bizarre that Audley felt confident that somewhere in the archives of military intelligence there would be a file and he could do worse than start with that.

His assumption was quickly proved correct. That Monday evening he excused himself from the Partners' Room and the customary cup of recovery to visit 25 Grant Street. The procedure for access to files was quite straightforward. One simply completed a form with all the relevant information and waited for its authorisation. The latter would include the location of the file, its reference and the time of attendance for its examination.

To Audley's surprise, he discovered that in order to satisfy his objective, he had to travel to Oxford the following evening and present himself precisely at 8 p.m. He looked at the young lady who had brought him the good tidings. "It's just as well I haven't got a social engagement."

"It wouldn't have made any difference." Her words were enhanced by a cynical half-smile. "You say what, and they say when. And that's the end of it."

"So it would seem." It was one of the occasions when Audley wished that he had the ability to conjure a short, sharp rejoinder that would leave him with the verbal break against service. But as always he was left with a tame return into the net.

Audley knew Oxford reasonably well. After all, he had spent three years at Balliol and had thoroughly enjoyed the opportunities and privileges of an undergraduate. Even so he could not recall Key Lane. Since ignorance is hardly the basis of punctuality, he decided to arrive in Oxford well in advance of the ordained time. It was just as well he did since it required several enquiries and considerable perseverance to find the correct address. Eventually he discovered it somewhere between Castle Street and New Inn Hall, which was a considerable surprise as he would have insisted that he was fully acquainted with that particular part of the town.

The house itself was cloaked in a thick mantle of ivy which straggled uncontrolled over window and door. Audley needed to part its tendrils in order to find the means of making his arrival known. A white button protruded from the oak door jamb. He pressed it. Despite his application of the appropriate sense and the advantage of the stillness of the evening, he could hear no response to his pressure. He pressed it a second time. That was a mistake. The door opened and a small figure erupted in front of him.

"What the devil do you think you are playing at? We knew you were coming so there is no need for you to advertise the fact. One ring is quite enough. I shall be obliged if you will remember that in future."

For the life of him, Audley could not decide whether the red face framed in a mop of unruly brown hair belonged to a man or woman. He, or she, wore a thick woollen sweater which rolled under the ears and down over the knees. At that level a pair of grey trousers linked the owner with two shoes that could hardly be called a pair. One was black and the other brown. Audley realised he was staring and there was every possibility he was now compounding his felony.

"I'm awfully sorry, I couldn't hear any bell so I pressed it again just in case."

"Well, don't do it again. It's quite unnecessary." The combination of hair, sweater, trousers and odd shoes turned around. It marched back into the house. Audley followed closely as he had no wish to repeat the process of entry.

The hallway was dark, first due to the absence of light and then further accentuated by the dominance of panelling and darkwood finish. The guardian of the house marched stiffly up the stairs, across the first floor landing and disappeared momentarily into an even darker void which Audley assumed was a room. A click followed by a somewhat yellow light encouraged Audley to complete the ascent and follow his guide. The room was not particularly large. Its dominant feature was a table of almost Dickensian structure. It reminded Audley of desks that he had seen over which Victorian clerks had leaned in the absence of stools in order to produce unblemished copperplate writing and figures beautifully underlined in red ink using round solid wooden rulers. He had a feeling that the latter must have been regarded as instruments of torture, not only in the physical problem of their use but also their availability as a means of punishment if the results achieved were unacceptable.

"I am Mrs Johnson." That, thought Audley, resolves that problem. "I understand you have an authorisation."

Audley pulled out his wallet and handed over the piece of paper. Mrs Johnson looked at it. "Right. If you will wait here I will be with you in a moment."

She was as good as her word. In less than a minute she had returned with a large brown folder and a sheet of cream paper. She placed the two on the sloping top of the desk. "Please sign this paper and record the time. I shall need your signature again when you return the file. In view of its classification, you are not allowed to take any copies or make any notes. I am required to stay with you as long as you have the file in your possession but I shall, of course, be at a discreet distance."

Audley could only imagine that she was referring to the discretion of ignorance. He merely nodded.

The file itself was extremely thick and heavy. There was no index but the pages were numbered top and bottom. The general impression was that its contents had been examined on a large number of occasions. It appeared to be set out in the in the form of a diary with commentary after each day's entries. The first page was headed '11th May 1941'. The Duke of Hamilton reported personally to the Prime Minister that he had had a visitor who had literally dropped in for tea.

The precise circumstances were that a Flight Lieutenant in the Luftwaffe had bailed out over eastern Scotland near a place called Dungavel. He had been apprehended by the local constabulary. Since he had sustained relatively minor injuries consistent with a parachute drop, he had been escorted to a miliary hospital near Glasgow. Up to that point in time he had insisted on answering questions simply with his name, which he gave as Horn, and serial number. Whilst he was being examined, he asked if he could speak with the Duke of Hamilton. Despite the natural denial of his request, he persisted and in the end identified himself as Rudolf Hess. During further interrogation, it seemed reasonable to assume that he spoke the truth.

There then followed several pages of commentary, with particular reference to the type of aircraft that Hess had flown and the problems that he had had to overcome in order to arrive so close to his ultimate destination. There was a suggestion that he might have flown a captured Spitfire to avoid the possibility of being shot down before he had attained his objective. This was discounted in theory, which was later supported by fact.

At this stage there were entries made at later dates in order to complete the chronological sequence. It appeared that the most likely aeroplane used was an ME110 which had the fuel capacity and equipment to enable it to make a reasonably safe flight adopting the same tactics as those employed in photographic missions. There was also a further comment, however, that provision could be made in such an aeroplane for a pilot and navigator, which would support the theory that Hess did not have the capability of achieving that which he intended as a solo operation. Reference was also made to subsequent interrogations during which Hess insisted that he had trained for the venture with the support of Willi Messerschmidt. Even with the benefit of hindsight, subsequent interrogation and the collection of evidence, the commentary appeared undecided on one major point. Did Hess in fact have a companion who was never traced? If he had such a companion, was he in fact Horn and could there be any possibility that Horn and Hess had switched places?

Audley paused for breath. The next entry was dated 12th and 13th May 1941. Not unnaturally, those responsible for counter-espionage had enquired of those in the highest of authority as to instructions. These were summarised in a number of memoranda including his treatment and complete isolation from any visitors except those determined by the Foreign Office. In particular he would be securely guarded and have no information as to events outside his confinement.

The next date of significance was 14th May 1941 during which Hess was interviewed for the second time. At this session, he gave the reason for his mission that he had an idealistic urge to arrange peace. He was quite convinced that he would find many sympathetic to his objective and in particular that the Duke of Hamilton would not only respond but introduce him to the highest authority in the land. He gave the reason for identifying the Duke as comment made by his political adviser, Karl Haushofer. The comment on these revelations was almost total disbelief. It began to raise doubts as to the sanity of Hess, although there was nothing in his conduct that could be taken to support such a conclusion.

The next entry was 15th May 1941 where Hess again confirmed that his was a peace mission and appeared to add nothing new to that which his interrogators had already discovered. The commentary was exceedingly short. It was, however, noted that Hess was confined to the Tower of London on 16th May 1941.

On 18th May Hess was transferred to a safe house at Aldershot. Instruction was given that he should not remain at the same address but should be moved at regular intervals to similar locations all within convenient reach of London. The only constant factor was the identity of the guardians to whom coded reference was made.

The next main entry was on 10th June when Hess was interviewed by Lord Simon on the instructions of the Cabinet. The significant result of that interrogation was omission rather than commission. After this particular entry, there followed an analysis which with the benefit of hindsight was able to relate events which were unknown in total at that particular time.

Audley managed to absorb this central theme.

As early in the Second World War as July 1940 Hitler had offered Britain a deal whereby if she returned Germany's former colonies the War could be ended. There had been no response. In the summer of that year, the Battle of Britain postponed Operation Sealion, the invasion of the United Kingdom, until the spring of the following year at the earliest. Hitler, meantime, had never taken his eye off the wheat and oil of the Ukraine. Russia was fully aware of her vulnerability and she had extended her air and naval bases during the second half of 1939, which position she further improved by attacking Finland, and in March 1940 acquiring additional bases. In August of that year, Russia had forced the Baltic states to become part of the Soviet Union, and Hitler could see his vista of wealth disappearing behind an impregnable defence. He decided that time was of the essence.

His plans for an offensive were temporarily suspended in recovering the ground lost by his Italian ally which involved the virtual control of Hungary, Rumania and Bulgaria and the acquisition of Yugoslavia and Greece.

It was not until April 1941 that Hitler had recovered that which had been lost and was no longer vulnerable to counter-attack. Unfortunately he had been obliged to destroy the British in Crete, but that was unavoidable since it had been used as a base for British bombers in attacking the underbelly of Europe.

The earliest point at which he could release Operation Barbarossa, the blitzkreig to end all blitzkreigs, against Russia was June 1941. On 22nd June of that year 187 divisions, together with some Finnish and Rumanian brigades, thrust deep into the heart of Russia and had advanced by the end of that year to Leningrad and Moscow. Hitler was at the peak of his power.

Comment was made on the fact that Hess appeared to have made no reference to these plans during his formal interrogations. Since the Prime Minister himself had issued instructions that Hess should have no communication concerning the conduct of the war and the German had commenced his incarceration confidently reiterating his sole objective was peace and thereby omitting any reference to the Russian strategy, nothing further of any significance seemed to have germinated.

Audley straightened his back. He had lost all count of time, but the state of his spine clearly confirmed that he had remained in one position far too long. As he streched his arms and back, he glanced across at the custodian of the files. He wondered whether from time to time she might be tempted to dip occasionally into the Stygian sea of half-truths, deception and deceit. Somehow he doubted it.

"Do you mind if I just walk up and down a little to stretch my legs while I think?"

"Not at all. Take as long as you like." The tone of voice was one of complete disinterest, but the twin reflectors which were it owner's eyes belied the casual reaction. She took her job seriously.

Audley tried to review what he had gleaned. There had been no mention of any letter or indeed any communication between Hess and any other party except those who had been briefed to interrogate him.

It was unlikely that more would be known to Military Intelligence than was actually recorded in the file. Despite the utmost endeavours and the benefits of access to German Military Intelligence records after 1945, there did not appear to be any new light shed on the conundrum. The general concensus appeared to be that Hess was Hess and that Hess was sane. There seemed to be no reason to doubt that his detention in Spandau followed exactly the same pattern as his detention in England during the war and therefore it was at the behest of the British Government. The fact that it might also be compatible with the intentions of the other Allies was interesting but irrelevant. So someone, somewhere, for some reason disbelieved Hess's story as it was recorded and was anxious that he should never have an opportunity of telling the whole truth and nothing but the truth. And that information could well be contained in the letter which had to be conveyed to the Duke who was expected to deliver it personally to the final addressee.

Putting together that which he knew before reading the file and that which he had obtained from it, the most likely theory would appear to be that the letter was related directly or indirectly to Operation Barbarossa.

Audley stopped pacing. He knew more than enough and was on the point of indulging in theorising.

"Thank you very much indeed, Mrs Johnson. I am sorry to have taken up so much of your time. Quite clearly, I will have to take advantage of your excellent service again and in anticipation, may I assure you I will only ring once."

Mrs Johnson stood up and sniffed. Words were superfluous and obviously for her a scarce commodity. She led the way downstairs and through the door in a silence which she maintained even in acknowledgement of Audley's farewell.

CHAPTER IX

Badminton

BADMINTON is a high spot in the Three Day Eventing calendar. It is also the ducal home of the Beauforts.

Audley found the annual round of Ascot, Wimbledon and Henley quite stimulating despite the vagaries of the so-called English summer. Horse riding events had never figured on his social scene and he felt an immediate antipathy when introduced to someone whose life appeared inextricably entwined with the antics of horses. The men were usually noisy, sporting both tweed jackets and M.F.H. number plates affixed to dark green six-wheeled Range Rovers. As for the women, he had found them to be even noisier than their menfolk. They enjoyed the reputation of being good fun at parties, emulating their equine idols in wild gallops and high-kicking antics.

"Jorrocks and Heigh-ho," muttered Audley as he left the M4 and followed the signpost to Tetbury.

The unsolicited invitation to attend Badminton would have been filed away in his wastepaper basket but for the fact that he had been intrigued by the hand-written note attached to it. This invited him to attend the Victorian Shadowgraph Tent on the afternoon of the first day and was signed "Carlton". Fortunately, Friday was quite acceptable as the alternative was a routine day in his City office. The Badminton Event lasted over three days and had he been invited to attend on Saturday or Sunday he would have been somewhat less sanguine in his acceptance.

The road required all of his attention. It twisted and turned up and down hill between thick hedges, the journey further impeded by the unusual density of traffic aimed at the one destination.

The car park was no more than a large grass field and despite the fine weather, it was already beginning to show signs of deteriorating into the inevitable bog which deterred more visitors than the organisers cared to recognise. Green wellies may well be an acceptable sign of social status, but their retention in mud after their owner has passed on is less a monument to society than an embarrassment to the would-be spectator, standing knee deep in mud minus their protection.

Badminton is more than a social event encompassing three days. It is a business, attracting many thousands of visitors who come to be entertained, which means spending money.

Their favourite day is that devoted to cross country and they position themselves avidly at those jumps where they believe from past experience that there is every probability that some of the contestants will come to a spectacular grief. Better still if their demise includes a ducking, since this compensates for their own wet discomfort. Before and after each round of the contest, the visitors retire to a small town of tents, especially erected for their entertainment, victualling and persuasion. All with the intent of relieving them of that heavy burden, money. These warm and dry sanctuaries range from the temples of bankers to the depositories of antique furniture.

But all offerings are enveloped in the shadow of their common idol – the noblest of beasts, the horse. Every conceivable appendage, accoutrement and attachment directly and indirectly related to that honourable animal is offered for sale. These are extended into paintings, prints, models and statues in every conceivable material whether mineral or stone. They are intended to grace table, wall, bonnet of car, or in the case of brass medallions even the walls of public houses and private loos.

It was the predominance of ladies that surprised Audley. He had been vaguely aware of their attitude toward horses, but he was completely unprepared for the range of age, apparently from cradle to grave, the disparity of substance and the extreme variance of female rump proudly displayed in stretch tight jodhpurs. He felt a momentary stab of panic which he quickly realised was quite illogical. There was no possibility that he might be overwhelmed by Amazonian cavalry who would trample him into the ever deepening mud. Like rabbits, the white tails, however awe-inspiring, were signals of retreat and not attack.

As is always the case in new and interesting surroundings, time had galloped on. He now had so little in hand that he felt obliged to seek directions to the Victorian Shadowgraph Tent. He had just summoned up his courage to tackle one of the less formidable pair of jodhpurs when he spotted a brightly coloured sign strung along the side of a tattered canvas structure that was on the point of expiring after years of constant erection and demolition. He paused at its entrance to allow his eyes to become acclimatised to the shadowy interior. The association of ideas was inevitable. For one moment he was the masterful sheik dominating an enormous harem. Those who day-dream risk the exposure of their thoughts by the opaqueness of their unrealised expressions. Audley's eyes and senses returned simultaneously to normality to discover that he was being viewed by a young lady with considerable amusment.

"Can I help you?" she asked. The inference was that she clearly thought he needed assistance in several ways.

"Oh, um, ah – yes, please." His response staggered down the steps from imagination to reality. "I would like a portrait or whatever you call it."

"A dense profile," she replied. Audley refrained from facetious comment.

"Yes, thank you. Can you accommodate me?"

"Of course. It will cost you £5 complete with frame. Is that all right?"

"Yes, thank you."

"Right then, sit in that booth over there. I will switch on this lamp. If you then do exactly as I say it will be quite painless."

The girl – she was in her very early twenties – wore a long floral dress which flowed from a tiny waist. The contrast with the army of marching jodhpurs was almost too much for Audley. Here was a real live woman, graceful and female.

"Please sit down in the booth." Audley realised he had been standing and staring. "Of course." He hurriedly did as he was told. "Not bad," he thought, "in fact, very nice."

The lamp blazed. His immediate reaction was to glance sideways at the source of light, which action he as quickly regretted. He could then see absolutely nothing.

"Please look straight ahead and keep absolutely still." The voice was sharp and precise. He wondered if she was a schoolma'am which was obviously the 'in' thing for young ladies in society. In which case her ambitions would reach far beyond his standing and means. Without hesitation he did as he was told. After about five minutes, the voice, this time much softer and relaxed, continued the instructions.

"I've drawn the profile outline, which I now need to fill in. It looks all right, but if you will stay there for just a few more minutes without moving I can then be quite certain."

Audley raised his eyebrows in acknowledgement then hurriedly dropped them back into the usual position. Although not particularly vain he did not want to distort what he hoped was a reasonable profile by wrinkling his flesh. He sat still. A minute or so passed, when another disembodied voice, this time male, but equally directorial opened fire in short, sharp bursts.

"Don't move. Stay exactly as you are and listen carefully. I am your contact with the Keeper. I will not repeat any of this so concentrate.

"I will list your priorities. First if you find the copy of the letter destroy it. Do not attempt to read, keep or pass it on. I do not want it. As your father before you, your mission is to be absolutely certain that it is destroyed but unlike him you will not hesitate even a moment. Secondly, if you cannot obtain possession of the copy, you will identify its location and ownership. That you will tell me when I ask and I will arrange whatever is necessary. Thirdly, if you become aware of some or all of its contents, whether the copy is destroyed or not, you will tell me exactly what you have learned.

"I hope that is clear. No need to answer. Finally, you can tell Clerkenwell everything you discover and I did say discover. From now on that which you know you will forget but that which you will learn, you will pass on to him. The vital element is the piece of paper. That no one shall have. Do not underestimate anyone whoever he is. Assume that everyone with whom you come into contact knows as much as you will do as a result of your enquiries.

"Never try to get in touch with me, even if you think you know who I am. Even in an absolute emergency you must use your ingenuity. The device is Greensleeves."

While listening to his instructions, Audley found that his eyesight was gradually returning. He wondered how far he could swivel his eyes without it becoming apparent to anyone watching his shadow. He decided to try. There was indeed a second profile on the sheet behind that of his own. He could just make out a dominant nose and a rather weak chin when suddenly it disappeared. Audley decided not to move his head although it was a reasonable assumption that his companion had walked away. He was beginning to appreciate the serious nature of his new vocation and the necessity to do precisely that which he was told. Nevertheless, there was some comfort to be gained in the knowledge that he had at least glimpsed the profile of his instructor.

He began to consider the phrase "the device is Greensleeves".

He hoped that his intelligence had not been overrated but he had a feeling that its meaning might defeat him. He had just arrived at this rather demoralising conclusion when the combination of the loss of bright light and the reintroduction of a now friendly female voice caused him to start to his feet.

"You certainly do as you are told. I wish I could say that about everyone."

Audley turned to face the young lady. He had to find out. "You sound like a teacher?"

"Ah, you think I am a governess and Daddy is Heathcliff! No, I am afraid I am one of the mass of unemployed. I hope eventually to make some money from my artistic talents but that's about as far as my commercial ambition stretches."

"So this was your idea?"

"Yes – and I must admit that it's not been at all bad so far. Of course the real test will be tomorrow and Sunday. If the weather's at all reasonable we should have the usual crowds and I shall stand a much better chance then of making some real money."

The emphasis laid upon the last two words suggested to Audley that whilst she might have limited commercial capability, her acumen needed no support. He felt he would like to know more.

"I wonder if you could show me the way to the refreshment tent. Perhaps you would like to join me in whatever they offer?"

"I am more than happy to give you directions, but I'm afraid I cannot leave this tent for the moment."

"Well, let me bring you something."

"That's very nice of you to suggest, but arrangements have already been made and you know what people are like. They get awfully upset if their intended good turn is pre-empted."

"Where are you going to pitch your tent again?"

"I am hoping to get permission around the corner, but at the moment I have no definite plans. I really wanted to see how this would go."

Persistence can sometimes be self-defeating. Audley decided that he had sent enough signals. If he were to establish any relationship it would have to be through his own initiative and on an entirely different tack. So he gave in gracefully.

"If you will point me in the direction of the watering-hole, I would be most grateful."

"Don't you want your profile?" She held out a white cardboard box.

"Of course, how foolish of me. You did say £5?" Audley

quickly extracted the note from his wallet and passed it to the girl. She handed him the box which he could see was open at one end.

"Aren't you going to have a look at it then?"

Audley began to feel somewhat uncomfortable. He could hardly pretend that he had any other reason for his visit to the tent than to satisfy his ego. He slid the small brown frame out of the box and looked quickly at the work of art. It was unfortunately extremely accurate. There was no doubt that he had at least one attribute in common with Royalty. His hair was remarkably thin on top. He replaced the frame quickly and without the slightest conviction said: "Very nice. I know exactly where I shall put it!"

The girl laughed. "You are the first person to say that but I am quite sure many others think it. Whilst we aim to please, kind sir, we do not aim to flatter."

Audley found her sense of humour infectious. As he followed her instructions, given clearly and without digital confirmation, he felt tempted to return before the conclusion of the Three Day Event. It was a possibility that had no future.

Despite his early morning start and lack of breakfast, Audley did not find the refreshments on offer particularly attractive. He decided to confine himself to a nondescript salad sandwich and a glass of dry white wine upon which any claim as to lineage would have been quickly denied. Having discovered the reason for his invitation, he could think of no immediate reason for remaining. Indeed, there were attractions to an early departure in that he would avoid a Moto-cross scramble that would inevitably ensue at the end of the day's activities.

The signposts to the car parks clearly pointed thc way, and he followed them in the vain hope that the route might accidentally take him past the Victorian Shadowgraph Tent. He had just arrived at a division between tents that made it clear that he was on the verge of the car park and, therefore, the failure of fulfilling his vague wish, when the sudden emergence of a group of apparently highly articulate but completely blind individuals immediately in his path obliged him to execute a side-step as neatly as any that he had performed on the rugger field in order to avoid direct physical contact. As he glanced around at those suddenly thrust upon him, half-expecting an apology, he suddenly realised that the man in their middle had a remarkably long nose and a very weak chin. He also recognised his face as one not infrequently seen on the society pages of expensive glossy magazines. The nose swung in his direction, flanked each side by a cold grey eye which was looking directly at him but appeared to be focused on some distant object. The absolute absence of even an acknowledgement of his presence, let alone recognition, was as clear a communication as an effusive welcome.

The knot of garrulous and self-contained status symbols continued their trot towards the fields of endeavour.

Audley drove home somewhat bewildered and considerably worried. He now knew the identity of his link; which information was both dangerous to himself and those to whom he was responsible. To make matters worse he was quite sure that his knowledge had been recognised.

Whatever the outcome of his visit to Badminton, his instructions from Clerkenwell remained and he would have to concentrate on a detailed recapitulation of Hess's visit. He decided to return to Grant Street on the following Monday to take advice on where to start and with whom. But the best laid plans of spies and men 'gang oft agley'. Monday was to be a day of unexpected developments.

CHAPTER X

Return to West Berlin

"THE Wall of China is rather like the Maginot Line. It looks good, it sounds good, but anyone can walk around it."

"So?"

"Everyone knows that as a defence it is a fiction so that no one believes that when the chips are down it is at all effective. After all, if you told me that you had a selling order today for Woolworths and you know I advise that company and I raised my eyebrows –" the speaker paused – "or didn't, then who is to say that a signal has passed or not passed?"

The two men were seated opposite each other, one leaning back in a tilting swivel chair at the working side of the desk and the other with his legs crossed in the inevitable high-backed leather armchair reserved for clients seeking pearls of wisdom which had a price and the seductive offer of possible riches. The word 'possible' was essential since in the tablets of the almighty ruler, stocks and shares could also go down as well as up. The constant repetition of such a statement suggested a need somewhat inconsistent with the 'word is my bond', 'breach of trust' and 'high performance units' laden atmosphere.

The occupant of the client's footstool was Audley. Facing him was the senior partner of the banking arm of the conglomerate that had been fused by the wealth creation forces generated by the greed of the Big Bang.

Audley considered his response. Words were always important. The use of tone, facetious expressions, even facial expressions was fraught with danger. Words would be repeated out of context and without any indication of their presentation, and words were more likely to be used to confirm failure rather than success.

"S'matter of fact, I can safely say I do not at this moment believe I have any substantial selling order for Woolworths or indeed knowledge of any particular interest in them one way or the other, so the problem doesn't arise."

Heatherington took the message. There was no point in labouring the matter any further. He had decided to refer to the purpose of the meeting when his telephone startled itself.

"Hello – it's for you – a personal call from Germany."

He made to pass the receiver across, but Audley was already on his feet.

"Tell her to transfer it to my office. I'll take it there rather than block your line. See you." The last words were lost in the closing of the door behind him. Heatherington looked at Audley's image with considerable astonishment.

"Maybe I was wrong. Perhaps we have a wall after all – no – sorry, I was talking to someone else. Would you please transfer this call to Mr Lonsdale's room? Thank you." He replaced the receiver slowly. It was a pity that the system did not allow internal connection without mutual knowledge.

Audley was relieved to find his own office empty. He sat at his table which he preferred to the leather-topped desks inherited by his partners and picked up the telephone. No point in attempting to guess. One sentence and he would know.

"Hello, Lonsdale speaking."

"Yes." The owner of the voice could have been in the next room. "Mr Lonsdale, this is Pluzes. We met recently. I thought I might take you up on your offer of professional advice. Can we meet fairly urgently? There is a development of which I would like to take advantage but I will need your assistance. The sums involved are quite substantial and your firm's return would be of similar proportions."

"Yes, Herr Pluzes. I remember our conversation very well. My firm would indeed be interested in helping you achieve your objective. What would you suggest?"

"Good. Well, time is of the essence and all the facts and figures are here in West Berlin. Could you visit with me – say tomorrow? I know you have many commitments but I can assure you that it would be a very worthwhile trip."

"Tomorrow is only possible if we can meet in the evening. I would then stay overnight and return early the following morning to London."

"Perfect. That would do admirably. We can certainly conclude our business in the evening and perhaps even have time for a little pleasure. May I suggest that I telephone your secretary tomorrow to confirm your flight which I will meet. I will also arrange, of course with your permission, suitable hotel accommodation."

Audley began to appreciate the sense of urgency behind Pluzes's calm impersonal voice. "Excellent. I will leave all the arrangements with you and I shall look forward to seeing you again."

"I also, and this time I hope we shall profit mutually by the combination of my opportunity with your knowledge. Auf wiedersehen."

"Thank you. Goodbye."

Audley looked at the ceiling as he pushed the telephone back to its usual position. Well, well, he thought, I wonder if Pluzes has found the letter or its present owner. And why does he need me?

CHAPTER XI

The Night Club

West Berlin

PLUZES had been as good as his word. All the arrangements had gone according to plan and the journey from office to hotel room had encountered less obstacles than the normal commuting struggle to cover some two score miles between the place of work and that of recovery.

Pluzes had behaved in the most unteutonic manner on their arrival at their hotel, shepherding Lonsdale through the lobby without bothering with registration. He had even insisted that Lonsdale's overnight bag should remain in the car for the time-being. This somewhat eccentric behaviour was soon explained.

"I have booked this room in the name of Benedict. We have a further room in your name at the Hotel Savoy, Fasanenstrasse. We will undoubtedly be under observation and they will have organised their schedules around your 'official' hotel. This temporary move will confuse them at least for the time-being. In addition, it is unlikely that this room can have been bugged as yours undoubtedly is."

Audley forbore to ask who 'they' were. He assumed that the K.G.B. or the East German Military Intelligence would be the answer.

Pluzes sat on the edge of the bed and motioned to Audley to take the only easy chair in the room.

"Right – I'll bring you up to date. I believe I know who has the copy letter. It undoubtedly passed through the hands of von Spuhler."

"So Frau Fischer did post it to Dietz and it was intercepted?"

"Yes. It's pretty certain Dietz never saw it."

"That makes sense – so who has it now?"

"Can't tell you until I'm certain. And even when I am, the

target is still the letter itself. And that's where you come in. I think I know how to introduce you to one of those who at least will be close to the letter. It is just possible that you may pick up some information which would only be available to you, but together with mine would give us both a much clearer overall picture. In other words, I have got as far as I can – you may be able to take it on. Are you willing to try?"

"Of course, if you think I can make something of it?"

"I am sure you can. It is only fair to warn you, however, that whilst you as an individual may be welcome, should your purpose become known your reception may turn very sour. Indeed it could be quite painful."

"Ah, well," Audley played the Englishman, "such is life. I'll be my usual vague self."

Pluzes was not even annoyed, let alone amused. "After we have eaten at your hotel we will visit the T. S. Elliot, which despite its name is a night club. They have one feature in the cabaret when they invite members of the club to assist in bathing beauties in specially prepared baths. You will volunteer for the first immersion."

"And then?"

"That's it. You will have the assistance of another member with whom I am sure you will have a most interesting night."

"And you?"

"I will disappear whilst you are performing. We will not meet again before you return to London, but I will contact you there when it is necessary. O.K? Any problems?"

"You are kidding. I'm by no means a virgin but visits to night clubs are not exactly an everyday event for me."

"So you will find it interesting. Now let us go to your hotel and get ready for the festivities."

The taxi deposited them opposite a doorway that dissolved under the bright glare of a thin neon tube, twisted to form the title 'T. S. Elliott'. Pluzes paid off the driver and then knocked sharply on the heavy door. A small slot appeared in it. No words were passed. Then, without the slightest warning the door slid silently from left to right uncovering a dark hole whose depth was given perspective by a square of white which hung suspended some three feet within it. Without hesitation, Pluzes walked quickly forward and Audley hastened to follow. The door slid swiftly back into place. This did not trigger off a blaze of lights and Audley had to wait to let his eyes become accustomed to the gloom. The white square was the shirt front of a huge gorilla stuffed into a dinner jacket. His frame blocked a further entrance which was protected by a heavy beaded curtain. Pluzes waved some slip of paper or cardboard. The gorilla swung himself to the left thereby allowing passage to the guests for each to pass one at a time through the curtain.

Audley was quite unprepared for the release of insulation provided by the apparently flimsy barrier. He was greeted by an ear-splitting, head throbbing cacophony whose sole musical content was the thump of drums reminiscent of tribal gatherings. The reduction of humanity to its lowest form of enjoyment and appreciation evidenced the victory of cunning over intelligence.

The T. S. Elliott was hardly the place for philosophy. It throbbed with noise, pierced from time to time by discordant laughter. It reeked of smoke, legal and illicit. It overwhelmed by disorientation and disturbance.

The first reaction was that it was a repetition of the night clubs that were rampant in Berlin during the 1930s. Even the most casual observation, however, confirmed that this was very far from the truth. The T. S. Elliott was not superficial. It did not provide a paper-thin façade for a society that was recklessly enjoying itself under the cynical eyes of those who sought to achieve power and domination.

The West Berlin night club some fifty years on was a more accurate barometer of the state of German society than its predecessor. West Berliners were wealthy. They enjoyed their food and drink. They liked to dress well and expensively. They liked to express themselves freely, which they could only do amongst their own kind. Their outstanding need was to confirm constantly and publicly their dominance over all. Deutschland uber Alles was temporarily restrained by one fact. Germany had been torn into two pieces. The desired Valhalla of German domination was inevitable when she returned to a single nation with a united people whose total resources and resourcefulness would ensure her the place she deserved amongst the world's super powers. There was no country in the world, including Japan, that could withstand the economic onslaught that a new United States of Germany could deliver as and when it needed.

In its way, therefore, the T. S. Elliott was just as much a façade as any of the clubs scrutinised by Christopher Isherwood, but the salient difference was that it fronted a self-confidence almost bordering upon complacency, arrogant wealth and a well-structured society that knew precisely where it was going and how it was going to get there.

The one advantage of letting his mind develop such thoughts was that it had given his eyes time to adjust completely to their new environment. They were standing at a long bar of unusual height and width. Audley appreciated that most Germans seemed to be taller and bigger than the average Englishman, but the bar still appeared to be quite an extraordinary obstacle to the full enjoyment of drink and the well-endowed young ladies who were endeavouring to keep all their customers supplied and happy. His confusion was further compounded by his companion's sudden acquisition of an additional twelve inches in height, thereby eliminating the problem of the exceptional measurements of the bar. The answer was quite simple: it was built on a plinth that acted as a substantial continuous step around its base. Audley mounted with relief. He could now see over the heads of those who were milling around between tables and apparently responding by sway and lurch to the throbbing pulse of sound.

"What would you like?" The words never existed. In company with the animal endeavours of the dancers, the drinkers had to resort to primitive sign language. Audley correctly interpreted the signals and pointed towards the appropriate bottle. Pluzes nodded and repeated the sounds suitably multiplied by a Churchillian gesture to the barmaid. Audley thought it extremely unlikely that a girl of her age would have had any understanding of the significance of the 'V' sign. It was probable that her generation had long ago absorbed the history of the Second World War as a betrayal rather than a defeat. In such circumstances there could never have been any victory.

Audley's eyes explored farther. The bar projected some distance into the room. There was a floor space, beyond which was a curtain which obviously screened the stage, which had to be extremely small. Pluzes had noted his scrutiny of the room and nodded. He was obviously confirming that that was it. The starting gate for Audley. He needed that drink. In fact he needed two or three but fortunately for him, Pluzes and good sense prevailed.

It occurred to Audley that being so far away from the stage might be a considerable disadvantage. At the critical moment, other suckers might volunteer before he could get there and as a foreigner he might well be unable to jump any queue. He motioned his intent to Pluzes, who nodded agreement. The two carefully stepped down to ground level and squeezed their way Indian file towards the end of the bar. Their progress was slow, sometimes painful from contact with elbow and foot and occasionally quite enjoyable through other anatomical contact, always of course with a suitable apology and a weather eye open for possibly churlish partners.

Despite his unusual surroundings and the abundance of interesting humanity, Audley found himself glancing at his watch. He motioned to Pluzes. "What time does the action start?" Pluzes indicated back: "Any time now." Audley shrugged mentally and pointed to his glass. Pluzes shook his head. "Better not" – or at least that is what Audley thought he said.

He returned to observing the peculiar actions of those around him. One young lady seemed intent on using her partner as a climbing frame. Another swayed backwards and forwards with eyes closed back to back with a tall, thin man whose flexibility was quite alarming. Audley could imagine some pleasure arising from the climbing of the first couple but the second appeared to merely affirm a unique case of mutual double-jointedness. Any pleasure it might give was quite beyond him.

He was beginning to extend his horizon to include a couple who seemed to prefer the top of the table, whilst three other individuals of uncertain sex filled the space underneath it, when the music changed or rather the thud degenerated into a series of taps that purported to represent a roll of drums. The show was about to commence.

Just to confirm matters, the curtain disappeared into the ceiling and a stage was revealed fully filled by another dinner-jacketed individual who resembled one of the lesser orders of the ape family. He spoke or rather shouted in truncated German. He was superfluous, unintelligible and unwelcome and he knew it. But he still had a job to do even if it was not appreciated.

"Ladies and gentlemen, welcome to the T. S. Elliott . . ." Like everyone present, Audley knew what the impresario was going to say and accordingly resented his insistence on saying it. The show was the thing and this man was no player. "May I introduce Stella." He stood aside to reveal a blonde young lady, clad in a brief bathrobe, carrying of all things a large plastic bucket. A towel of miniscule proportions was slung over one shoulder.

Someone somewhere must have pressed a button. A trap door in front of the stage opened – fortunately no one was standing on the precise spot – and an old-fashioned tin bath rose into glorious view. The bath itself was set on a small platform with steps at either end. It continued to rise until its edge was about four feet from the floor.

Stella walked across from the stage on to the platform and then, still wearing the robe and carrying her bucket, stepped into the bath where she remained, aloof and apparently oblivious to the acclamation and greetings of those who had paid to be entertained. Her indifference had the same root as their interest. Money. Her view of humanity was that of herself. Everyone had his or her price dependent upon the cost they believed they suffered. A customer paid ridiculous sums for titillation; she received ridiculous amounts for providing their satisfaction. The same shade of colour painted on the original merges and disappears when it dries. For Stella, the only reality was the pay cheque each night. For the customer the only reality was the final settlement.

"Now, gentlemen, who would like . . ." Audley started. He looked at Pluzes for support and finding none, moved forward, pushing his way with unnatural disregard for others. His efforts were rewarded. The disturbance drew the eye of the master of ceremonies.

"Ah, here we have . . ." The rest of his remarks were lost in the general appreciation of Audley's response. Amongst the laughter and noise he heard the occasional surprised comment, "He looks like an Englishman." How on earth could they decide that? he thought, as he arrived at the foot of the steps. Hands pushed and prodded him to discourage the slightest pause between lateral and vertical motion. He accelerated up on to the platform to avoid the growing intimacy of the prodding. The throng jostled nearer and more noisily. The master of ceremonies indicated to Audley that he should now remove the bathrobe.

In order to achieve this he had to stand behind Stella, which he accomplished by sliding carefully around the bath, being conscious of the inches available for his large feet. He had noted that her belt was loosely twisted, so he assumed all he had to do was to pinch the robe on each shoulder between thumb and forefinger and then lift.

His logic was absolutely right, but he had forgotten that Stella still held her bucket in one hand. There then followed a series of scenes that would have filled the theatre year after year. In the first instance the robe was removed entirely except where it covered the arm that held the bucket. That rose vertically, spilling the contents of the bucket, an assortments of brushes, cloths, soaps and miscellaneous items, into the bath, together with the towel which had adorned Stella's shoulder. From his vantage point, Audley could see the effect of the warm water on the objects which were obviously essential parts of the entertainment in their original state. So he bent forward to try to retrieve them. As he did, the level of his arm holding the robe descended. The robe began to absorb water by capillary action. The props were fast degenerating into a sodden mass that would be of no help whatsoever in the primary purpose of the act, the bathing of beautiful Stella.

In his anxiety to salvage something, Audley had found an aerosol can which he gripped, inevitably in the wrong place. A cascade of white form erupted into Stella's face, which came to life with remarkable alacrity. She became aware of the possibilities of the situation and responded accordingly. Had the action followed its usual course with the manipulation of brushes, loofahs, soaps and cloths and things, she would have disembodied her mind and only returned to her human frame at the conclusion of the entertainment. Being an object of sexual desire, even if that implied some visual abuse, had a certain positive quality. At least she had a desirable body, which fact she knew to be true. But to be the unwilling nude partner of a Laurel-and-Hardy-type feature was to be ridiculed. Any female body would suit such a purpose, and hers was not just anybody's. She slapped Audley. It was inevitable, but for him quite unexpected and inexplicable. He slipped and grabbed Stella to avoid falling off the platform. She staggered, put one foot on the remains of a piece of soap and fell backwards into the bath. Audley was thrust forward over her head into the bath. The audience was treated to the vision of a hooded female head emerging at one end of the bath apparently connected (albeit out of sight) in the water to a very wet pair of male trousers that cycled their way up into the air.

The laughter was hysterical. Audley's head appeared in the middle of the bath to be greeted by a shower of blows from a brush that forunately seemed to be made of quite soft plastic material. Nevertheless, it was a far from comfortable experience, made complicated by the fact that he had his back to his assailant who had locked her legs around his waist. His groping hand discovered the bucket. He had no alternative. He placed it over his head to act as a protective helmet. It worked, but had one major disadvantage. He could not see.

The audience hooted. Stella belaboured the bucket. Audley sought to untwine her legs. Since he still retained some of the inhibition of a gentleman which precluded him from taking the ultimate advantage of the position in order to free himself, he was quite unsuccessful in his efforts. That left him with only one alternative. He stood up – with difficulty it is true, but nevertheless with success.

The club was in an uproar. Stella had given Audley best and had disappeared back into the bath. He stood like a knight of old, apparently emerging from some lake to save his love, with a plastic bucket over his head, the handle as a chin strap, the end of the robe in one hand and an aerosol can in the other. He still could not see, so he dropped the can which bounced off the huge head of a spectator who was so painfully convulsed with laughter that he was quite unaware of the cause of the lump which would need careful explanation the following day.

With one hand free, Audley could then remove the bucket. But at that moment Stella decided to recover her modesty so she pulled the robe – hard. Audley disappeared sideways into the bath, bucket dislodged. He seriously thought of relaxing under the water and quietly slipping into the next world. It was becoming increasingly difficult to decide which was the more painful, that which he was suffering physically or the mental distress of humiliation. He suddenly recalled that, with the exception of Pluzes, he could at least retain the mask of anonymity. To remain where he was would be to increase his unnecessary suffering, so he gritted his teeth, gripped the edge of the bath and in one movement climbed out and fell down. He had forgotten that his foothold on the edge of the platform was only a matter of inches.

The next few minutes were but a blur. Willing hands helped Audley from the scene of his triumph into what he decided must be the manager's office. He recovered to find himself seated, a soggy heap in what was normally a comfortable chair quite unprepared for a saturated occupant. Audley rubbed his eyes. His hair was still acting as a conduit for the water dripping down his head. As his vision improved, he realised that there were two men at the far end of a desk. One was seated and the other was standing to his right.

"I wonder if either of you two gentlemen has a handkerchief I can borrow?"

The man who was seated pulled a drawer out of the desk. "We can do better than that, here is a towel. I have asked the staff if they can find some clothes that might fit you. We will have yours cleaned and returned to your hotel in a matter of hours. I hope you will accept our apologies for the inconvenience, and of course if you have suffered any damage, we shall be more than happy to pay whatever is necessary."

"Oh – that's all right. It was entirely my own fault. I was carried away in the first place and I deserved to be carried away in the last!"

Neither man smiled. It was probable that they were not at all happy with a possible change in reputation of their establishment from one of sexual satisfaction to that of farcical entertainment. Like all good businessmen, they knew precisely the most profitable service they could offer. The fact that their present audience had thoroughly enjoyed themselves was irrelevant. They knew that however profitable innocent fun and games may be, it had no comparison with the return that might be achieved through the sale of sex. There was a knock on the door and a young man entered bearing a bundle of clothes.

"Perhaps you would like to change in my bathroom?" The man who had been originally standing at the far end of the desk had walked out into the centre of the office. He pointed towards a panelled wall. Audley correctly guessed that a section could be opened to afford entry into a most luxurious suite. He availed himself of all its facilities and some twenty minutes later emerged thoroughly refreshed.

"Ah, that's better. Your friend is waiting outside in his car. We'll make sure that all your clothes are back with you in good time this morning. You need have no worries on that score. Once again, if there is anything we can do to recompense you for your inconvenience, please let me know."

There was now only one occupant of the office. He was still seated behind the desk as if he were a permanent fixture. Audley expressed his thanks and seeing only one door, decided that that must lead him to his meeting point with Pluzes. As it turned out, he had no problem in locating the exit since as he emerged from the office, he was gently herded by the gorilla guardian along a narrow corridor through a heavily barred door into the cold morning air. A black BMW crouched on the opposite side of the road. The door of the club slammed shut behind him and he felt rather like a prisoner ejected from jail, unwelcome and unwanted. He walked across to the BMW and opened the passenger door.

The driver was not Pluzes. Nevertheless he seemed to be expecting Audley.

"Please get in. I realise there's not much of the night left, but perhaps we can make good use of it." Audley paused and then decided to accept.

The car accelerated rapidly and the driver turned towards him. "Do you know West Berlin very well?"

"No, I am afraid I do not."

"Well, perhaps that's an advantage. If I were you I would relax and take five."

Audley correctly interpreted this as a suggestion that conversation and navigation were being discouraged.

The car swept smoothly on, an interesting example of German engineering. Audley tried to recall the advertisement that he had often seen on television which began with the word 'Durch'. He was unsuccessful. Despite the recommendation, he did his best to note buildings and landmarks they passed, although he knew he would be hard put to repeat the route at some later date if so required.

Without any warning, either to his passenger or to any possible traffic, the driver turned the car sharply down a ramp which ended in the basement of a very large block of flats.

"Well, here we are. If you would like to follow me?"

Audley allowed himself to be conducted up a series of stairs. When he expressed some surprise that there was no lift, he was curtly informed that they had no desire to wake up the concierge. He had forgotten that it was now well into the early hours of the morning.

Eventually they arrived at the fifth floor according to the black numeral painted on the white wall of the staircase, and pushed through a fire door back into the civilised carpets and wall-coverings of the formal passages. His guide knocked gently on the door numbered 521. After the briefest pause, the door opened inwards and a beautifully manicured hand gently waved at Audley.

"Please come in as quietly as you can." The words were in English and their enunciation was perfect. Nevertheless, Audley was convinced that the invitation was not extended by one of his countrymen. He turned to thank the man who had so safely delivered him, but he had already disappeared. Audley shrugged and did as he was bid.

The room was heavily curtained so that it needed the many lamps that were scattered around in the absence of ceiling lighting. His host was dressed in the most magnificent crimson smoking jacket, a well-pressed cravat and equally sharp trousers. His slippers were of tooled leather and he gave the overall impression of fastidious perfection. It was the eyes that gave him away. They snapped like a pair of laser beams, focusing with intent and deliberation yet at the same time missing nothing on the periphery of their concentration. Whilst his general appearance conveyed the possibility that he might be gay, homosexual or bent, it in no way distorted the overriding impression that he was a very dangerous man. Audley began to wonder who he was.

The thin face twisted into a wry smile. "You are wondering why you are here? Well, the answer is very simple. I felt I should take advantage of this visit to Berlin in case you do not return for some time to avoid any possible misunderstanding that might otherwise arise. I am Pluzes's control. I know that he arranged for you to meet someone this evening, and for reasons which were unpremeditated that did not happen. To compound this omission, Pluzes has not reported, which we previously arranged he should do. I have reason to believe that he has some information that will put him at risk and unfortunately he did not have the time or the opportunity to pass it on to me. It is just possible that he may have told you. If he has, and you do not tell me, you will be as vulnerable as he is and I regret to say in all probability you will join him wherever he is. Therefore, it is very much in our mutual interests that we should both know everything that you know."

Audley had a tremendous feeling of déjà vu. He had no reason to disbelieve that argument. "I understand precisely what you mean. To the best of my knowledge and belief Pluzes did not tell me today anything other than what he had previously told me. However, to make sure I will endeavour to recall precisely everything that he said and you can take your pick."

The nod confirmed the agreement. Audley sat down and did his best to fulfil his promise. This took him about half an hour, at the end of which instead of the expected barrage of questions, there was a long silence.

"Pity. Now we shall indeed have to start all over again." The man seemed genuinely sad. Audley was sure, however, that it was nothing at all to do with Pluzes, rather the fact that information had been gained and lost. "It is just possible that whoever was supposed to meet you at the T. S. Elliott will, in fact, get in touch with you. Somehow I doubt it, as the meeting was arranged in Berlin and you will be going back this morning to London. Nevertheless, if you receive any contact in any form whatsoever which you feel might have the slightest connection with this evening's activities, then I would like you to contact this man in Haslemere."

He handed Audley a small business card which was that of an academic. Surprisingly enough, considering the address in Haslemere, Surrey, the title and the qualifications were in German, as indeed was the individual's name, Muhler. Audley carefully put the card into his wallet.

"I will not pretend for one moment that I can ask you not to disclose whatever you might discover to your own control, but I would suggest that you mention to him our conversation and get his approval of my request. Then we shall all be happy." Audley looked at his watch. It was nearly five o'clock and he was really committed to the early morning flight. His action was not unnoticed. "We will now take you to your hotel where you can change into your original clothes and refresh yourself. I am afraid you will have little time to sleep, but doubtless you will be able to make up for that later on this week. I think it highly unlikely we shall ever meet again, in fact I might go as far as to say I hope not for both our sakes."

He held out his hand, which with some reluctance Audley gripped. He was right – it was rather like shaking hands with a wet fish. For all his faults Clerkenwell suddenly became almost attractive.

CHAPTER XII

The Bait

SEATED opposite his control, Audley began to revise his views concerning Clerkenwell yet again. The man was obviously no idiot and he was obliged to be concerned with every minute detail. Nevertheless, Audley had recounted every second of his visit to West Berlin on five different occasions and on one had actually had the pleasure of listening to his taped replies to identical questions on consecutive interrogations. He had never claimed to possess total recall, but was beginning to regret his retentive memory. The more details he produced, the more were expected.

"Very unsatisfactory." Clerkenwell had said this on every occasion. "Obviously, Pluzes was getting near to the truth but he did not take the simple precaution of keeping his control fully advised."

Audley knew precisely what was coming next. It was a lesson for him to learn at somebody else's expense. "I am sure I do not have to repeat it again." Audley was surprised. "However, you should learn it as an object lesson for which somebody has paid an extremely high price." Audley's surprise evaporated. It condensed again into wondering how often the process was to be repeated. Unwittingly, Clerkenwell provided the answer to that particular question.

"Let's move on. Muhler is a retired professor of modern languages. He came to this country in 1952 and we have had him under general observation as an agent for a 'friendly' nation. He seems to have confined himself to businessmen who might go behind the Iron Curtain pursuing their normal activities and has used the German trade mission for that purpose on a number of occasions. We believe that he is now relatively harmless and is merely a communication channel. We therefore have no objection to you telling him what you and I agree."

Audley then decided figuratively speaking to stick his neck out.

"I have been thinking. This saga started when a copy of the letter surfaced. That copy had been kept by the secretary who produced or had produced the original. There must have been an official copy. That would have been kept in Hitler's secret files. It has always been assumed that these were burned."

Clerkenwell interrupted. "I don't think there is any doubt about that. When the Russians were attacking Berlin, the Führer himself destroyed his private papers before poisoning and possibly shooting himself and Eva Braun."

"Yes, but there is no definite proof. The fact that on the same basis a copy letter appears, is enough to suggest that in the absence of absolute evidence any possibility could arise."

Clerkenwell gave his beard three swift tugs. His eyes were fixed on Audley. "If I am right, what you are suggesting is not that we look for such a copy but that we pretend we have found it?"

"Precisely. No one knows what Pluzes had found, so what would happen if it was generally assumed that he had found another copy?" There was a moment's silence, then Clerkenwell spoke quietly.

"The proverbial would hit the fan and he who ducked last would get a face full." Audley was not quite sure what it meant but it sounded significant. He felt in the circumstances that it would be politic not to respond.

Clerkenwell continued to massage his beard. "But how to make it sound probable. You have told German Military Intelligence that Pluzes told you nothing. We could argue that you would not tell them anyway until you had told me. In which case, I might then say you could tell Muhler on the basis that two organisations were better than one, particularly if Pluzes had found it in Germany."

"Yes, I think that might work."

"Now let's rehearse what Pluzes told you."

Audley leaned back in his chair. "It can either be a brand new line of enquiry or it can have a connection with that which has gone before. A completely different approach might be suspect as being too coincidental. However, I would go for an unexpected development following his original enquiries."

"I agree. Suppose he had researched Frau Fischer's husband and found that he was present in the bunker during the Russians' last onslaught on Berlin. No – that would not work because he would then have both copies. Let's assume again that he had a colleague in the bunker but neither was at all certain that he would survive so they each had a copy. No, that's a bit too much like a boy's own paper. Let's suppose again, however, that Hitler entrusted the files of the Fourth Reich . . ." Suddenly Clerkenwell paused. Audley watched him closely. He was obviously getting very excited. Something had occurred to him which had opened up a flood-gate of possibilities.

"That's it. Of course, I had forgotten completely. The Fourth Reich and U124. Now we have the key to the whole puzzle. I can tell you precisely what Pluzes said to you and you can then relay that equally precisely to Herr Muhler, sorry Professor Muhler, and then stand clear. It will get very exciting."

Audley listened extremely carefully, first conscious of the need for memorising that which he had been told, but soon from sheer genuine interest. The possibilities were exciting and needed no repetition. Nevertheless, Clerkenwell insisted that at the end of his pronouncements, Audley should repeat the story to him, word for word and be prepared for a considerable number of questions. It was nearly midnight before they had finished, but each was satisfied that their new story held together.

"You know," said Clerkenwell, "I do believe it happened already!"

Audley laughed. "It could easily have done. Perhaps what we imagined is no more than fact."

"In which case we might eventually be somewhat embarrassed." Clerkenwell relaxed into a more thoughtful mood for no apparent reason. Audley stood up. He had to put in an appearance the following morning at the office even though he could not claim that the workload would be onerous. It was hardly worth while returning home. He would go by his club just in case they had accommodation, which would be extremely convenient.

CHAPTER XIII

The German Agent

HASLEMERE boasts the longest platform on the old Southern Railway other than Waterloo. This simply arose because the directors of the company lived in that fortunate town and therefore required all expresses to stop in order to ensure swift and comfortable passage to their London office.

The town itself is quite charming; somewhat overwhelmed by a new supermarket, but the joy of its inhabitants lies in its trees and the glorious surrounding countryside. Audley tracked down Professor Muhler simply by looking in the telephone directory. The address listed was in Derby Road, and that was just as easy to find, being quite close to the station. He had, as usual, opted to travel by car knowing that it would be a very pleasant mid-week drive.

The Professor was a little rotund man, reminding Audley of a chipmunk. His eyes were bright. He was round-shouldered and leaned forward clasping his hands together hard on his chest. On the few occasions that these parted company, Audley expected to see a shower of nuts released to cascade over floor and table. On each occasion he was disappointed.

"Ah – yes, Mr Lonsdale. You telephoned me this morning. Please come in."

Audley had decided to make his visit as brief as possible. It was, after all, supposed to be formal.

"I have some information for you, Professor Muhler. I understand you will be interested and I have been instructed to pass it on to you." Audley emphasised the word 'instructed' and hoped that Muhler had duly noted the fact.

"A gentleman I think you know, a Mr Pluzes, became aware of some facts which he passed on to me the other day. They are somewhat complicated so you may wish to take notes."

"That is very kind of you, but I have no need because I think we can record what you say if you have no objection."

"No, that's perfectly all right with me." Audley paused to allow Muhler to obtain his equipment, but the latter made no move. Obviously the recording had been intended with or without agreement. "Right. The facts are these which, with your permission, I will dictate for the benefit of your machine." Muhler expressed his thanks very softly.

"First, a large number of files identified by the letters VR were collected and prepared for shipment on U124.

"Secondly, amongst these files was private correspondence which was in file number VR77A.

"Thirdly, for reasons that are not immediately apparent, that particular file was abstracted with the intent that it should be retained in Europe, whereas U124 was intended for the Far East.

"Fourthly, VR77A was handed over to a Herr Sperrhake with instructions for its translation to microfilm and destruction of the original. The storage of the microfilm was to be the responsibility of cell B13, which operated in Bavaria.

"Fifthly, in that file was the original copy of the letter from the leader to his opposite number. Since this is being recorded I would prefer not to use names that are already known to you, if that's all right with you." Professor Muhler nodded.

"Sixthly, whilst that cell was exclusively committed to German Military Intelligence, Herr Sperrhake was not. Pluzes had reason to believe, therefore, that he had abstracted the copy letter and it did not appear on the microfilm. Sperrhake passed the letter on and we believe the recipient at that time lived in Passau.

"Lastly, the key to Pluzes's discovery was the absence of the letter on the microfilm and his conclusion that the only person who could have taken it before reproduction was the courier himself. I believe that we were going to meet someone from the cell, but that is only conjecture. Everything else is fact as told to me by Pluzes."

Muhler had been sitting as though hypnotised. He cleared his throat. "But you mentioned none of this when you were in Berlin." It was not a question but a statement.

"Of course not. I had no means of knowing whether the chap was in fact what he said he was. In think he understood that, because he suggested that I could get confirmation of what he said before I spoke to you."

Muhler made no comment. He stood up and waved his arm

towards the window. "I enjoy a beautiful garden. It is beginning to look quite colourful again. Before I offer you a cup of tea, perhaps you would care to take a stroll, that is if you like gardens?"

Audley was somewhat taken aback. He had expected a host of questions and not immediate acceptance. As they walked across a beautifully prepared lawn, Muhler apologised for the state of the rose bushes.

"Whilst it is a great joy to wake up in the morning and find the deer in your garden, it is a mixed blessing. They particularly enjoy my roses and so do I. The only problem is, I prefer to see them whilst they obviously enjoy their taste. The lower half of the garden is relatively uncultivated, but I have some magnificent hydrangea bushes. Perhaps you would care to see them."

He led the way between some magnificent oak trees which defended about half his garden against human intervention. The trees looked down over a multiplicity of bushes and shrubs which twittered and shook with contented bird life.

"I have no recording apparatus here, and anyway it is I who wish to talk. I will of course relate precisely what you have said and indeed any other comments you wish to make. I leave it entirely to your discretion, as I have no alternative, as to how much I may say you wish to pass on.

"The situation is extremely delicate. I have a great regard for your country, but a devotion to my own. I have no doubt that we are both aware of the circumstances surrounding U124. In fact it was one of five 'U' boats commissioned to take certain important people, considerable funds and vital information to a number of safe locations in preparation for a new beginning.

"By a means which we have never truly identified, the British Navy were able to intercept and sink U124 so that its contents were never recovered. Again, I am sure you have a very full dossier on the history of that particular boat. The partition of our country in 1945, however, meant that a completely new strategy had to be constructed, and it was not simply a matter of reorganising, regrouping and then re-emerging as a political party. Only recently has it been realised that there was a vital use for that which has been set aside for the Fourth Reich in the possible cementing of the division between East and West Germany. This became even more obvious when nuclear disarmament, particularly of short- and medium-range weapons, lost its identity as an orphan and has become a prodigal son.

"As a result of your endeavours over the last few weeks you are privy to a scenario that previously could not have been known to more than, say, six people in the whole world. Even they would not have known the identity of each other. In addition to yourself, I am now added to that group. I do not wish to be part of it. My only objective in life is to enjoy in peace and solitude the few years that I have remaining. I am tempted to suggest that we never met, but the only way I can be absolutely certain of that is to kill you. Twenty years ago that I certainly would have done. Today, perhaps unfortunately for both of us, I could not regard it as a satisfactory solution."

Muhler was becoming increasingly agitated. He began plucking at leaves until he unintentionally grasped a thorn which drew blood. He cursed in German which clearly demonstrated the extent of his concentration and distress. For him, it was obvious that Audley was no longer present. After about ten minutes in this state, Muhler adjusted himself to the present.

"I shall tell my superiors that I had no need to continue our conversation as I am fully aware of the facts surrounding U124, and the data you had given me was very precise. I did not wish to prolong the interview because I did not want to reciprocate, and that would have been unavoidable had I subjected you to question and answer. That may satisfy them, but what they may do next will not be affected at all by whether they believe my explanation or not."

"What do you think, then, will be their next move?"

"Probably I shall be recalled immediately to Germany, and the best I can hope for will be a quiet secluded place in Bavaria with absolutely no visitors permitted other than those nominated by my masters." Muhler shrugged his shoulders. "In one way that would suit me very well, so it would not be unwelcome even though I shall have to leave this beautiful garden."

"And what about my masters?"

"They certainly will not be interested in me. As far as you are concerned, they will let you run until they are sure that they know everything that you do and you have uncovered everything you possibly can."

Audley correctly assumed that Muhler was referring to Clerkenwell and his superiors. He hoped that he represented a somewhat greater value to those he owed an ultimate allegiance. Nevertheless, the situation was far from encouraging. Muhler seemed a little bit more relaxed.

"So you think that there may be room for negotiation?" asked Audley.

"It is possible. Your people would probably still have the last say in any new approach to the U124 and we might be prepared to trade the copy letter to our mutual advantage, say the destruction of both."

Audley could see no advantage in prolonging the discussion. He glanced at his watch. "I think I will return to town. That is unless you have any other suggestions."

"No, I think we have gone as far as we need. I am under instruction to report this evening and there will be no way I can delay that. I would suggest you get your report in at the same time, so that neither side feel that they have any advantage, as that may not be advantageous to us personally."

Audley nodded. "Well, nice to have met you. It looks unlikely that we will meet again. I hope you will enjoy your garden for some time to come wherever it may be located."

"Thank you very much. I hope you have many years to enjoy whatever suits your fancy."

On that pessimistic note, the two men shook hands and went their respective ways, one back to his house and the other to his motor-car.

If Clerkenwell slept, it could only be at his office. It seemed whatever time of day Audley was desirous of reporting to him personally, he was available. Whether this was exceptional, Audley did not know. Nevertheless, he was impressed by his control's dedication.

"Well?" Clerkenwell had not allowed him time even to cross the threshold. Audley refrained from replying until he had seated himself comfortably.

"Well, Muhler took the bait without any hesitation or indeed question."

"No questions? That is interesting. So you didn't learn anything new?"

"No, it seemed to fit in perfectly with that which he already knew and he didn't ask for any clarification or explanation at all."

"Probably because he didn't want you to ask him any questions." Audley mentally made a note that his assumption with regard to Clerkenwell was more than correct. He was not a man ever to be underestimated.

"It could well be. Anyway, I think the hook is firmly fixed and the fish is up and running. Is there anything further I should do?"

"No – except to let me know immediately – and I mean immediately – anyone contacts you. You are not to agree to any meetings or any arrangements or communication without my prior approval. When someone does get in touch with you, find out as much as you can without giving anything away. This stage has to be handled with the greatest possible care and constant liaison."

"Understood. I will let you know immediately I hear anything at all." Audley stood up to go but Clerkenwell held up his hand.

"Before you take your leave, however, just to make sure we have got everything absolutely right, I would like you to record in depth your conversation with Muhler, following our usual practice. Jenny will arrange whatever is necessary."

For the first time Audley had difficulty in putting together a clear and precise résumé. On several occasions he had felt exceptionally tired but that was to be anticipated and understood. Now a new element had been introduced. There was the stress of remembering what he had to forget and then recalling that which had been forgotten. There was now the strain of knowing more than he should and deciding whether that information could be forgotten in total. Finally, there was an element of fear which had been inculcated by a succession of reminders that he was by no means indispensable to everyone, and it only required one exception of the general concensus to ensure his premature demise. Audley suddenly felt very tired. He would have an early night for a change.

CHAPTER XIV

Asprey Appears

THE insanity of the dealing-room was a welcome return to normality. The shouts and cries of eager young men on the Exchange floor had been replaced by the urgent mumbling of the new generation. This consisted of young men and women staring hypnotically at monitor screens whilst repetitively punching buttons as a means of digital exercise and communication with the latent beast to which they were permanently attached.

It was rumoured that the average salary was in excess of £200,000 per annum coupled with the equal conviction that every penny of such an exorbitant sum was well and truly earned. The persons so paid were expected to be available twenty-four hours a day on the basis that the modern instruments of torture linked markets around the globe, so that there was forever a shaft of sunlight spotlighting the frantic efforts of humans intent upon buying or selling at a profit.

There was a time when Australians enjoyed the reputation that they would bet on anything, a characteristic obviously inherited from their forebears who, as convicts, spent long periods of confinement with no other means of passing the time. Englishmen, as befits a superior race, do not gamble. They speculate. The difference between the two in theory was that to gamble was to take an unknown risk whereas speculation is decision-making after the elimination of all the uncertain elements.

In the good old bad old days of stockbroking, it was not uncommon, particularly in the provinces outside London, for brokers also to be jobbers. In short, they bought or sold on behalf of their clients but themselves maintained the 'book'. In such circumstances, there was no doubt whatsoever that the brokers had eliminated every possible risk other than the bankruptcy of their client. It was equally certain that their clients, entirely without realisation of course, were emulating their Australian cousins.

The principle of professionalism was added to persuade the more cynical that even where a broker was not in a position to 'make the market' he would not take advantage of the client by buying and selling in front of him. The obvious temptation was there. If the principal took advantage of specialist knowledge to buy or sell shares, then his agent could play the same card first, rather than follow suit.

To the outsider, it is quite inconceivable that a man of knowledge and experience should encourage others to enjoy the consequent benefits of that combination in preference to himself. In practice, the broker does remarkably well by a series of recommendations that are in fact self-fulfilling. An outstanding example of such acumen was one Jim Slater, who achieved the penultimate rung of the City ladder, promoted by the greed and avarice of others.

To Audley, stockbroking was a business in which his family had invested originally their resources and subsequently their time and energy with remarkable and consistent success. Much emphasis had been laid upon the salaries of those newcomers whose dealing skills were apparently essential to the continuity of the Big Bang. The essence of the Establishment is that it will pay almost anything out of profits, provided a substantial surplus remains.

A practical translation of that was eventually made public in the case of Lloyds, when it became known beyond the Golden Mile that the simple practice of sub-underwriting and/or insurance was an extremely useful means of accumulating personal wealth rapidly and free of tax. The fact that it was also possibly illegal and certainly immoral was no advantage. It did not, however, act as a deterrent.

Morality and money are incompatible, a philosophy clearly understood and promoted by those who believe in the sanctity of humanity despite the consequence of inevitable poverty.

It would be quite untrue to suggest that any of these ponderous thoughts crossed Audley's mind as he entered the dealing-room. The familiarity of the activities within it was enough to cause him to relax and wish for one fleeting moment that the meeting at the Carlton had never happened. He shrugged his shoulders as soon as the thought crossed his mind. Wishing away was even more futile than wishing for. One problem of being the boss is that every move and mood is observed and interpreted by the subordinates.

"The market is very firm, sir". The speaker was a bright young man who had decided that Audley's shrug was one of disinterest and if left unchallenged could not auger well for those engaged in it.

"Glad to hear it – Tyzack, is it not?"

"Yes, sir. I look after the oil market. Looks as though OPEC is managing to keep its act together."

"Good." Audley was not sure whether he could comment further without revealing his ignorance. "Jolly good show." He had taken the coward's course. Tyzack's eyebrows rose as he opened his mouth but before he could cast any more pearls, Audley had started to retreat. He had decided that he would return to his office where, although he might be at the mercy of the telephone, he would not be required to participate in his firm's internal relations.

The prescribed reading for the day was already on his desk and his secretary had followed him in with the very desirable cup of coffee which she prepared with great alacrity immediately he appeared in her office. It was difficult to assess which of her many contributions to Audley's comfort was appreciated the most. Whatever the sequence of priorities, there was no doubt that the ubiquitous cup of coffee figured highly on the list.

"Any particular appointments today, Miss Harford?" Audley always insisted on formality, at least within his office.

"Just the one, Mr Lonsdale." Susan responded in like manner.

"I expect that is at lunch?"

"Yes. James Lowther and you are hosts to the Chairman and Chief Executive of the Radio company."

Miss Harford tended to identify clients by the occupation rather than by name. That tendency probably arose because she was half Welsh, who because of their limited vocabulary in surnames, qualified them to permit precise identification. It was also rumoured that such a nomenclature assisted in establishing the pecking order in the chapels, the anticipated donation on the plate and the general social acceptability of persons so named. The advantages were so clear that it was the very last classification that the English would ever adopt. They preferred to preface their identifications with titles that had absolutely no connection with trade or profession but were rooted in status, prestige and recognition.

"Ah yes. The knight and his shining armour. It should be a very pleasant lunch. The company is doing exceptionally well and enjoying our advice. In addition the Chairman is excellent company." Audley quickly glanced through the correspondence laid before him. "Are there any messages?"

"Yes, two. One from Sir Edward, are you free on Saturday afternoon? He has to attend a charity cricket match and would like someone to share the burden with him. The other is from Gemma and she asked if you would give her a ring."

Audley responded automatically "Thank you". He decided he would telephone both that evening. "Nothing else?"

Miss Harford deliberately paused to emphasise the fact that had there been she would have told him. "Not that I am aware of."

And so it remained. For some two weeks Audley had reverted to his usual round of work and recreation. The days began to accelerate and merge as his routine was reinstated.

He had decided to travel by train to and from London as statistics and experience combined to suggest that he was on the verge of a major accident on the M25. It required more than strong nerves to enter that combat zone morning and night, and despite the apparent convenience of door-to-door mobility it was becoming increasing a battle that could only be lost. It was simply a question of time.

Fortunately for Audley, his commitment was such that he could literally afford to travel at a convenient time and in a comfortable manner which allowed him to catch up with his reading. It is customary for a commuter to either participate in group therapy en route to and from his office, or to seek isolation in the cocoon of his work or daily newspaper. Audley fell into the second category quite naturally. He was therefore not a little annoyed and somewhat abrupt when his private defenses were breached by the traveller sitting opposite him.

"Sorry to interrupt. I am sure we have met before. Never forget a face, but names are a different matter. Did you go to Ascot last year?"

Audley placed his forefinger deliberately in the middle of the page in front of him. To those so tutored, the message was clear. He regarded it as a temporary invasion of his privacy, one that he would quickly repel and then return to his occupation.

"I am afraid I cannot recall either your face or your name. I certainly do occasionally go to Ascot but . . ."

"Odd, that. I could have sworn you were the chap who made a bundle on that horse in the third race, what was its name? Ah, Greensleeves, I think."

Audley froze. Had he been more experienced in such matters,

it is likely that his reaction would have been less obvious. As it was, it caused the man seated opposite to him to glance around quickly. Audley recovered himself. "You may well be right. I certainly recall that. My name is Lonsdale."

"Ah, good, my name is Asprey. I don't think you've heard of me."

"You're not connected with the . . .?"

"No, I have no business in England."

"Well, in that case, you are quite right."

"I wonder if you could spare an hour or so this afternoon?"

"Yes, I think that can be arranged. Where would you like to meet and when. At my office?"

The stranger shook his head. "No, thank you very much. May I suggest here at 3 o'clock?" Asprey had drawn an invitation card from his inside pocket and was busily writing on it. He handed it across to Audley who recognised it immediately. It was an invitation to attend on a Peer of the Realm at the House of Lords. Asprey chuckled.

"No that's not my other name, but he has kindly suggested that we might use his facilities. If you will present the card then they will look after you. I take it you have been there before?"

"Yes, on several occasions."

"Good. I shall look forward to seeing you then this afternoon. Sorry to have interrupted your reading."

Asprey then unfolded his newspaper and held it in front of his face. Audley glanced down at the tip of his forefinger; it had become white from the pressure unwittingly thrust upon it.

A reception at the House of Lords is a most uplifting experience. It is very pleasant to be able to instruct the taxi driver, to be virtually lifted out of that vehicle by the policeman on duty and then to float inside to be received by the most courteous lackeys in the land. Those who seek to enjoy that experience in the absence of a formal invitation should not be fooled. The elegance of attire is but a thin façade. The unwelcome guest is the recipient of a bum's rush that would do credit to many a more lowly rated club in Soho. To those who are there by right or invitation, however, the atmosphere is unique and self-indulgent.

It was true that Audley had visited the sanctum on several occasions, and being the second son might one day even be invited to attend in his own right. This possibility added a certain spice to his enjoyment.

He was directed up the red-carpeted stairs to the library. To his surprise, however, he found Asprey standing at the head.

"Follow me." Audley did as he was bid and, via a series of corridors, finally found their destination, a small suite of rooms to which he was a complete stranger. Asprey motioned towards one chair whilst he took the other.

"I am afraid I have not ordered anything because I thought that we ought to get down to business straight away, and we don't want any interruptions.

"Now, I am interested in a certain letter and a particular vessel which at this point in time is lying on the bottom of the ocean somewhere. You know to what I refer?"

Audley was concentrating almost painfully. He conveyed his understanding without overt sign.

"For reasons which I will not go into, whilst we have retained the method of communication – that is, we come to you – we have changed the channel. In future you will report to me." Audley was not surprised. He had anticipated that possibility since he had become aware of the identity of his link. So he said nothing.

"Now I want you to repeat everything you know from your conversations with your Military Intelligence control, Pluzes, his control and Muhler. I am not going to record anything, neither is there any device for that purpose here, so, I will ask you to be as clear and concise as possible."

Audley began with his visit to Berlin at the behest of Pluzes and ended with his report to Clerkenwell. Asprey interrupted on several occasions to require further clarification on points of detail. It was obvious, however, that he was fully conversant with the overall position. When Audley had stated that he had finished, Asprey jumped to his feet. He issued his instructions as he paced across the carpeted floor.

"You will tell Clerkenwell that you have had a telephone call at your place of business. It is extremely unlikely that your firm will have any taps. The caller identified himself as a friend of Professor Muhler. You will tell Clerkenwell that this caller said that a deal could be done whereby the copy of the letter will be destroyed in your presence if U124 was destroyed with one of his representatives present. The timing and arrangements are entirely with you. You will be given a week in which to test whether the principles are acceptable. If they are, then you and he will agree the arrangements. The man said he would contact you again, but did not indicate how or when. Is that clear?"

"Perfectly. Very simple."

"Not so. To persuade Clerkenwell, who is by no means a fool, you will need to imagine the conversation precisely, and I would suggest that you mentally replay my voice and what I have said as if it were on the telephone. Then, however innocent the question, you have the answer."

Audley took the point. It was becoming increasingly obvious that attention to detail was the difference between success or failure, and the latter would be extremely painful.

"May I suggest that you find your own way out? It should not be difficult, and if you are challenged en route simply tell them that you are looking for the exit and whom you have been visiting. Do not, of course, mention my name."

Audley felt that he would welcome Miss Harford with open arms if she suddenly appeared with a cup of coffee, which he sorely needed. He followed his instructions to the letter and commanded a cab to take him back to his office as quickly as possible. There he 'phoned Clerkenwell and arranged to walk around to Grant Street as soon as he could conveniently leave his desk.

The tip that he should imagine the telephone conversation as a reproduction of Asprey's instructions proved extremely helpful. Clerkenwell appeared to accept all aspects of the message as being genuine, although he questioned Audley very closely on several points.

"Good. To continue your metaphor, we now have to land the fish." Audley looked at him with some surprise. "I thought your prime objective was the destruction of the paper?"

"Yes, it is; but I think with a bit of luck we may use a net as well as a hook with some good effect."

Audley did not like the sound of that. If Clerkenwell was going to try to take advantage of the situation, however friendly and co-operative German Military Intelligence might appear to be, they would not enjoy any unnecessary exposure, particularly any dramatic transition from their natural element to someone else's dry land.

"I am not sure," he said, "what you are trying to achieve?"

"True," said Clerkenwell cheerfully. "Perhaps we should confine ourselves solely to our given objective."

Audley was not convinced, but there was little he could do about it. Not only was the next event ouside his control but it appeared that the consequences would be equally unaffected by his influence or intention.

CHAPTER XV

Asprey Starts Fishing

THE next development took Audley completely by surprise. He had been invited down for the week-end to stay with his elder brother, who had inherited the family estate as well as the title. Despite a large number of bar sinisters, which if nothing else evidenced exceptional virility, each generation had managed to produce a male heir and therefore adequate succession.

There had been and remained constant debate as to whether seniority by age necessarily ensured the passage of competence and intelligence, and Audley had often expressed grave doubts on that score. Nevertheless, there was little else he could do about it, and kind hearts and coronets seemed too drastic an approach simply because fate had dealt him as a second card.

His arrival at Beaumont Manor was via the front door, but that was the extent of ceremony. His brother, John, boasted a butler who doubled as a chauffeur and occasionally trebled as the gardener. The butler's wife endeavoured to fill the corresponding female roles in addition to the satisfaction of her husband's demands. She was quite busy.

John and Audley had had a sister but she had unexpectedly died at an early age, a regrettable departure as she had not time enough to demonstrate any particular traits or capabilities other than those associated with a very young child.

John, known as Lord Meany to his associates and family, attempted to sustain the material wealth of his empire without undue effort, which was compensated by the unnatural devotion of his bank manager.

The elder brother enjoyed field sports. He hunted; that is to say, rode a horse. He shot; to be more precise he pulled the trigger. And he fished; wet fly of course. In short he was a patient man, content with his lot. The contrast between the two brothers was simply expressed in terms of talents. John had one in that he happened to have been born first. Audley had several of which he needed some reminding. Exploitation was in the vocabulary of neither of them.

An unavoidable part of the week-end ritual was attendance at early morning service in the local parish church. Whilst any comparison to Sandringham would have been quite misplaced, the attendance of the Lord of the Manor still held a certain cachet for those who regarded church attendance as a means of being seen.

There were two routes to return to the manor for Sunday lunch. The first was via the local pub and the second along the stream that meandered between the village and the ancestral home. John and his wife Mary inevitably took the former. For that reason alone Audley decided on the latter.

In fact he thoroughly enjoyed the walk and wished that he could encourage the self-discipline necessary to get up early in the morning and enjoy the undoubted delights of the countryside. It was a repetitious self-criticism that as usual was quite ineffective. He was completely unprepared for the interruption of his thoughts.

"Good morning, or rather good afternoon."

Audley started and looked around. There standing in the trees away from the river bank was Charles Asprey.

"Oh, how do you do? Surprised to see you here."

"Yes. You are not an easy chap to pin down in some quiet place."

Audley felt rather like a butterfly, but made no comment.

"Have you got agreement to the principles we discussed the other day?"

"All is agreed."

"Good. That is good."

Asprey walked down the slight slope until he was within a yard of Audley. "Now we can agree arrangements." He pulled a long manila envelope from inside his coat. He handed it over to Audley. "I am sure Clerkenwell can arrange what is required in this envelope. He will need to enlist the help of Naval Intelligence, the Foreign Office and to some extent, the Diplomatic

Service. That sounds an ambitious list, but in practice it should be quite straightforward."

"I have been thinking about this," said Audley. "I am a little confused. How can *we* . . ." And he emphasised that word, "*we* deliver the goods? I understood that the copy letter is with the Germans and well beyond our influence."

"You are partially right. It is with the Germans, but we, unlike Clerkenwell, have some influence. We, in fact, are mediating, and although Clerkenwell would never know it, we will succeed where he can only fail. However, yours is not to reason why."

Audley hoped that the rather infantile phrase required no further conclusion. "Very well. I will give this to Clerkenwell. Do you suggest that I open it?"

"On the contrary, I would recommend for your sake that you tell him that you have been instructed not to examine its contents and that you have obeyed those instructions to the very letter."

"And how do you suggest I obtained this envelope?"

"As before. You tell Clerkenwell the truth with the exception of my name and my facial description. If I were you I would describe your brother, which shouldn't be too difficult. Now you and I will probably not meet again so I will wish you well."

Asprey did not attempt to shake hands. He inclined his head and then walked quickly back into the trees. Audley stayed on the river bank looking at the slow-moving stream. A flash of light caught his eye and he saw reflected on the surface a beam that seemed to bounce towards the hill which overshadowed the stream on the side opposite to him. There was another flash of light and with it the realisation that the meeting between himself and Asprey had not gone unobserved. Whatever the implications of that fact, it served to endorse Asprey's suggestion that he should stick to the truth with very little deviation.

At luncheon table Audley was not particularly good company, and it was with mutual relief that he decided to return to his more modest accommodation at the conclusion of the meal.

He had decided not to telephone Clerkenwell but to go to Grant Street first thing on Monday morning rather than leave it until the evening of that day. As he had anticipated, Clerkenwell was there before him and received the envelope with considerable eagerness and satisfaction. He listened carefully to Audley's description of the meeting, the only variance from the truth being that of Asprey's description and the only omissions being his name and the probability of an observer. Audley had decided that if it was one of Clerkenwell's men, it would be better for Clerkenwell to feel that his insurance had been effective. If, on the other hand, it was someone with an entirely different interest, he would only start a hare that might inadvertently lead to an embarrassing conclusion.

It was soon obvious that Clerkenwell had no intention of sharing the contents of the envelope with Audley. Having expressed his thanks and congratulations, he pointedly waved Audley out of his office, at the same time instructing his secretary on the intercom that on no account was he to be disturbed.

Audley walked back slowly to his office wondering whether he had at last seen the end of his assignment. Somehow he doubted it.

Audley's forebodings were completely with foundation. Only three days after his meeting with him, Clerkenwell telephoned.

"We have the green light. If it is possible, we would like you to go to a little place called Selb, which is in Bavaria, next Tuesday. You will need to fly to Frankfurt and there catch a feeder plane which will take you direct to that town. Can you make that?"

Audley opened his diary merely as a precaution and glanced at the following week's commitments. "Yes. I need only make one small adjustment provided I can get there and back in a day."

"That should be quite reasonable. It will mean an early start. I will book the flights and arrange the tickets and have them sent round to you on Monday."

"May I ask the purpose of the trip?"

"Simply to meet some people, one of whom you've met before, your friend Spuhler, to see if it is possible to do a deal along the lines we've discussed."

"Is that all?"

"For the moment, yes. If there is anything else I will put it in the evelope. If you have any further queries, just pop in to see me."

Audley had once visited Passau and he could recall the sweeping fields and woods leading to the foothills of the Alps. He doubted whether he would have either the time or the inclination to enjoy Bavarian geography on this occasion.

CHAPTER XVI

Bavaria

AUDLEY joined the file that snaked across the tarmac towards the DeHavilland Otter. He counted eight passengers including himself, but it was the size rather than the number that gave him food for thought.

The cabin of the aeroplane accommodated passengers in two rows. That on the left-hand side facing the front consisted of single seats, whereas there were two rows on the right-hand side which purported to provide accommodation for normal persons. Since normality is an average between two extremes, it is comfortable for one and virtually impossible for the other. Audley had no doubt that the Teutonic frame constituted the upper end of the spectrum, and his forebodings were more than justified. Good manners, often absent when Germans board an aeroplane but prevailing as far as he was concerned, confined his choice to one aisle seat. Unfortunately, this necessitated him sitting next to a lady who overflowed in every conceivable direction. Consequently he was obliged to impede the progress of anyone who wished to go beyond his row.

His dismal anticipation was confirmed by the natural desire of the two pilots to enter their cockpit, which was only possible after traversing the cabin. Fortunately, both the young men were of extremely slim proportions so that their passage through was just physically possible.

Audley blinked. Whilst the aeroplane belonged to Lufthansa, the pilot and co-pilot would have been more at home in the Luftwaffe. Both wore black uniforms, carried high-peaked black flat hats and wore what appeared to be black riding-boots. Both were blond, blue-eyed, narrow of feature and brimming with self-confidence. Each carried silver-framed sunglasses. They obviously rode on arrogance. It was this latter attribute that caused Audley to fasten his safety belt.

The Otter sported two turb-charged engines and was renowned for its short take-off and landing capabilities. The pilots left no doubt in the minds of their passengers on that score. The small plane quivered at the end of the runway, leapt forward and within a matter of yards was airborne, climbing steeply, turning sharply at one and the same time.

Unlike most civilised take-offs, the relationship between Frankfurt and the aeroplane remained constant. It was only the speed of their exit from the city that confirmed to Audley that they had indeed left the ground and were flying.

As he afterwards discovered, the flight from Frankfurt to Selb, a small town in Bavaria, was known as the tree-skimmer. Whatever the weather conditions, the aeroplane flew at less than 2,000 ft and therefore avoided certain responsibilities as to flight planning and programming. It also enabled the pilots to demonstrate their uncanny ability to avoid obstacles by either going around or under them in preference to going over. It was an interesting experience cushioned only by the massive inflatable companion whose presence assured Audley of at least a soft landing.

Even this was to be denied him. Selb airport was a single grass strip that was elevated and therefore subject to cross-winds, which were further accentuated by tall trees that added to the rural charm of that part of Germany. The plane approached the field flying at an angle of 45 degrees to the runway, both engines screaming in defiance and assuring all who were prepared to listen that they would resist to the last moment the intentions of their master. Audley had had previous experience of Lufthansa flying Boeing 737s, but there was no comparison. He would have preferred experience in the Fleet Air Arm but even that would not have prepared him for the final manoeuvre. Approximately six inches above the grass, the pilot applied violent left rudder so that the plane's direction was more natural in relation to the field and then switched the engines to reverse thrust. The result was a supreme example of the excellence of timing. Everything about the approach had been wrong. It had almost been irrelevant. Yet the final touch-down was a demonstration of the mastery of all elements and the supreme competence of those responsible for it. At a more mundane level, Audley's hopes as to the cushioning effect of his companion were completely dashed. The Otter and the ground collided.

Since the majority of the passengers wished to disembark either because they had reached their destination or the limits of their nerves, Audley allowed himself to be ejected on the basis of last in, first out. He walked towards a building that obviously served as the airport's facilities. As he arrived at its entrance, he glanced at the car park in its rear and recognised the figure of Herr Spuhler standing alongside a red Mercedes. The industrialist raised his left arm which Audley took as the signal that he might be approached.

Spuhler opened the passenger door and then walked around the other side of the car. The two men looked at each other across its roof.

"You may not have enjoyed it, but I am sure it was an experience." Spuhler was smiling with apparently genuine amusement.

"It will be interesting to see his technique when we come to land at Frankfurt. I would hope there he will be obliged to conform."

Spuhler shrugged and laughed. "Let's go."

Within a few moments of leaving the airfield, Audley began to wonder whether the Mercedes was simply a reincarnation of the Otter. He looked sideways at Spuhler, half expecting him to be wearing a peaked cap flattened over his eyes, as his approach to driving was frighteningly similar to the method of flying from which he had just escaped. The road, although wide and smooth of surface, wound between forests and undulated in such a manner that forward visibility at high speed was non-existent. And Spuhler drove very fast indeed. The climax of the journey, if it could be so called, was when the German decided to overtake another Mercedes which was meandering along at a mere 110 m.p.h. in the middle of a sweeping bend, when it was clear to see that the speed of approach of an oncoming car was such that there was neither time nor space for such a manoeuvre.

The two vehicles thundered towards each other like medieval knights on chargers intent on proving their manhood. The other car flashed its lights. Spuhler grunted approval. The other car braked and slewed wildly yet apparently still under control. At this moment, Spuhler was alongside the Mercedes that he intended to overtake. Audley saw that driver's head lurch forward as he applied his brakes. The net result was the avoidance by the thickness of two cigarette papers of a fusion of metal and humans at a combined speed of some 300 m.p.h.

Spuhler grunted again. "As soon as he flashed I knew he would give way."

Audley could not restrain himself. "And if he had not?"

Spuhler shrugged again. "They always do."

Audley mentally added the rider "at least so far". He could imagine exactly the same conversation with the two younger men who had literally dropped him in from the skies. The self-assurance was frighteningly close to absolute arrogance. In its presence, the only defence was fatalism. Audley relaxed and attempted, quite unsuccessfully, to view his predicament philosophically.

Selb is a small town dominated by ceramics or porcelain. Southern Germany is the home of many crafts and skills. Some arise from centuries of specialisation including musical instruments of considerable international renown. There are other industries that rely more on natural resources but still require exquisite skill in their translation of very mundane lumps into objects of considerable beauty.

The concentration of these crafts had encouraged the continuance of a paternalistic society which in a way was almost feudal in its structure. The boss was the master with considerable power over the lives of those he employed. The owners of businesses took more than a passing interest in the leisure activities of their employees. This was not regarded as an intrusion in their privacy, and the workers themselves welcomed the totality of their involvement.

Audley was generally aware of the situation from his previous knowledge of Germany, but had never before had the opportunity of seeing first hand how the system operated and the people that enjoyed it. He assumed that Spuhler had an intimate knowledge. After a few questions he found that to be so and was encouraged to enquire more deeply.

"This, then, is rather an isolated part of Germany?"

"Not at all. It is the heart of Germany. The foreigner often assumes that Prussia provides a profile of the true German. Nothing could be further from reality. Bavaria is the source of power whilst other parts of Germany are the sources of wealth. If you like, Bavaria is the diplomatic centre. The source of continuity."

Audley was about to turn a translation of these general principles into facts when Spuhler stepped viciously on the brake pedal. They were approaching the brow of a hill and the combination of excellent engineering and gravity enabled the driver to reduce his speed dramatically as the Mercedes continued in a straight line.

The cause of Spuhler's remarkable reaction rose above the sky-line. It was the head and shoulders of a helmeted soldier, which projected from the turret of a huge tank thundering its way up the opposing side of the hill, occupying practically the whole of the width of the road.

Audley had a vision of an angel of death straddling a huge machine which proudly bore the insignia of the black iron cross. The Panzer made no attempt to deviate, and it was entirely due to Spuhler's remarkable driving ability that the Mercedes and its occupants survived by leaving the road and rejoining it without significant harm other than mud on the one and perspiration on the other.

Audley thought, "E'en the ranks of Tuscany could scarce forbear to cheer". Whatever the heights of their arrogance, there was no doubt that when the chips were down, the Germans had some justification for their attitude.

"Does that kind of thing happen often?"

"Often enough. The army prefer this part for their manoeuvres because of the terrain and the amount of space there is available to them."

Audley made no comment on the use of roads and indeed decided to refrain from extending that subject further.

Spuhler glanced at him. "We are going to the hunting lodge of a company that specialises in porcelain. It has dominated Selb for many, many years and is indeed the largest employer in the district. Its product is internationally famous. What is not generally known, however, is that it has made Meissen products under licence since the division of Germany. That will show you the excellence of their workers."

"I did not realise that East German products could be made in West Germany under licence."

"Of course. Why not? We are the same people and we have the same skills, but we also have greater resources. Finally, we do not suffer from weak currency but rather can take advantage of our position to pay royalties in Deutschmarks which our friends find very attractive. You will also discover that as you enter the lodge, there are samples of products that have been made by the Selb company for many years alongside Meissen products which have been made both in East Germany and under licence here. The quality is identical throughout."

They were now driving much more slowly along a narrow road between heavily wooded hills and Spuhler almost slowed to a walking pace as he turned the car between two posts that heralded the approach to a hunting lodge. The distance between the road and their destination was extremely short. Spuhler parked his Mercedes alongside several other gleaming monsters and motioned to Audley to follow him through the main entrance. As he got out of the car, Audley glimpsed a broad stream languidly flowing between the trees and adding to the already idyllic surroundings. The lodge itself could well have been a setting for the Prisoner of Zenda, and put the equivalent of the English kings to shame. It was built mainly from timber, with leaded windows and extremely ornate shutters. Wood carving appeared to be as strong an occupation in Bavaria as it was in such centres as Nürnberg.

Audley, however, was not given the time to absorb his surroundings. Spuhler had disappeared very quickly into the lodge and he was obliged to follow without further hesitation.

The reception area was as he had been warned, a showroom of porcelain pieces of many shapes and sizes. The predominant colour was blue. Whether the utensil was designed to go under the bed or in the centre of the dining table, the decorative finishes were remarkably similar. Again, Audley was unfortunately pre-empted in any further examination by Spuhler waving to him as he pushed his way through a green baize-covered door. "This way." The other entrance was into the workers' restaurant and leisure rooms. "This is our meeting room."

Although sunlight streamed through the trees outside, the drawn shutters successfully obliterated their assistance in illuminating the room, which relied entirely on a number of lamps supporting the main chandelier. There were two men standing in front of a tapestry. Spuhler walked towards them and Audley dutifully followed. Spuhler introduced Audley to the bulkier of the two, but made no attempt to do likewise for the other.

"Herr Lonsdale, this is Herr Sperrhake. He has some questions to ask you and some information. I hope you will be able to talk freely. Please let me know when you are ready to leave. We have no specific timetable so you need not worry about time." Spuhler turned away from him and bowed towards the two men who had remained silent, spun on his heel and left the room.

Herr Sperrhake motioned to Audley to sit down. The three men then relaxed in a small circle of chairs which were actually far more comfortable than they appeared. Audley waited.

"Thank you for coming. We have no desire to detain you any further than is necessary, and it is essential that we should have no misunderstandings between us. I realise that your German is excellent but we will conduct our conversation in English. You have my assurance that we are not taking any record whatsoever."

Audley felt obliged to say "Thank you".

"We are led to believe that you have certain information concerning a file that was copied on to microfilm before it was destroyed. That there was one document in that file that was not microfilmed but abstracted. Am I right so far?"

"Yes."

"Good. Now I must tell you at the outset that I do not believe that story in its entirety. It may well be that the contents of a file were microcopied. If that had taken place, however, the original would have been returned so that a complete set would have been shipped. Permanent extraction of any document would have been quite impossible. The contents would have been checked with the utmost care before release and upon return of the file. Having said all that, however, we wish to be absolutely certain and this is where we look to you for help."

"I think I understand, but may I suggest that before we get down to the specific problem you might relieve me of a certain disadvantage. I also wish to be absolutely certain and therefore not rely upon guesses or assumptions. Who precisely are you, or more accurately whom do you represent?"

Herr Sperrhake acknowledged the correctness of the question. "I quite understand. You will have every right to ask and I am obliged to tell you. My colleague and I represent an organisation which is not dissimilar to your own. And I am not referring to that in Grant Street. There is in fact a significant difference. To begin with, we have not been in existence, at least as a unified whole, for the centuries that you have enjoyed. Secondly, we have been consistent and managed to avoid, as far as we know, infiltrators, imitators or usurpers. The irony, however, is some of our roots became intertwined with yours, and for a considerable period our respective organisations were in conflict. However, the First World War put paid to that, since when you have virtually eliminated our influence in your country and we have reverted to two distinct entities with quite different objectives.

"Finally we are obliged to retain a much lower profile in Europe than you need to do in your country and we have far less power and influence particularly whilst Germany remains two separate countries." Sperrhake paused. Audley had understood in broad principle what he had been told but was still not quite clear as to the bargain that he was being offered.

"Would it be at all helpful if you introduced your colleague?"

Sperrhake shook his head. "I think not. He is here as an observer because he knows better than anyone what was in the files about which we are concerned."

Audley looked at the stranger with increased interest. He guessed him to be in his late fifties or early sixties. His white hair contrasted with his very brown skin. Audley guessed that the man's tan had been acquired through many years of living in a country where the sun was less of a stranger than in most of Europe.

"If you say so. Now to put my cards on the table. We, and I am not referring to Grant Street, know that a certain letter was written by the then leader of the nation, addressed to an individual of some authority in another and that that letter was destroyed.

"We now believe that at least one copy was retained and that that surfaced within the last few months. We are also concerned at the possibility of yet another copy. I would emphasise that our anxiety is related to existence and ownership of these copies and not to the knowledge of their contents. I am under instruction to obtain them or to be absolutely certain that they have been completely destroyed. The contents without the copies are mere speculation."

The two Germans nodded. Sperrhake responded. "That I understand. Our position, however, is slightly different. The value of the letter to us is also that it provides proof positive of its existence and therefore the information it provides is incontrovertible. Having read it, as we have, we can understand why you do not wish it ever to be published. We could not care less. But it is your desire that governs our reaction."

Audley began to see daylight. Herr Spuhler had obviously passed the copy produced by Frau Fischer to Sperrhake and the organisation he represented. They were perfectly aware of the value of the letter and it was going to be simply a matter of price. He decided to try to find out what they had in mind.

"I have the authority to offer you anything within reason for the copy letter or the absolute certainty of its destruction. I can see no alternative as far as the second is concerned to my being present when it is destroyed. However, that is a detail. The immediate question is what are you prepared to accept as consideration for either?"

Sperrhake looked at his colleague and raised his eyebrows. Obtaining no response, he faced Audley again.

"I am afraid it is not as simple as that. If you will bear with me I will explain why not. In 1945, despite your best endeavours in which I will admit Churchill took a leading hand, the Western Allies were somewhat remiss in driving across Europe and certainly Germany itself. I grant you that the counter-offensive in the Ardennes was not particularly helpful, but even so your lack of progress enabled the Russians to come farther into Germany than they need otherwise have done. The result was the partitioning of our nation and the creation of two states with all the dissipation of resources, willpower and effort. In short, an utter emasculation of our once great nation." Sperrhake's voice had risen in tone and in strength. His companion coughed. Sperrhake heeded the interruption and visibly relaxed.

"But that's all history. Nevertheless, whilst we cannot put the clock back, the time is fast approaching when unification is a practical possibility and politically acceptable. In order to achieve it within a reasonable time, however, we need to use everything at our disposal. As you know, our main thrust is to persuade the Russians that we can commit the Allies to dismantle their nuclear armaments by creating a nuclear-free barrier between East and West. The larger the barrier the more effective it will be, and this can best be attained by the unification of West and East Germany into one nuclear-free zone which has allegiance to both sides or to neither, whichever is deemed to be more appropriate.

"The current progress of talks between the two super powers presents us with a potential problem. That which we offer might be less attractive as agreement follows agreement and, whilst it is very unlikely the Americans will hand over and dismantle their Strategic Defence Initiative, they might still discover that our bargaining power has been reduced below an effective level. Hence our present wish to retain as many cards as is possible and fortunately for us and perhaps unfortunately for you, this is one of them."

The penny had dropped. Audley clearly understood the position. The German Establishment held Frau Fischer's copy of the 'H' letter. It had no intention of destroying it, neither was it willing to sell it to anyone at that stage. When the time was ripe, however, it would be produced as one of the means of encouraging the United Kingdom to support unification of Germany. The German Establishment would also have an alternative strategy. It might well be that the Russians would also like to know the precise contents of the letter, the identification of those named in it and therefore those that they would still regard as their enemies.

Sperrhake seemed to be able to read Audley's thoughts. "I think on the whole it would be worth far more to the British than to the Russians, but even that lesser value might tip the scales as far as our objective is concerned."

"May I therefore summarise what I understand you to have said. I would very much like to be absolutely certain that I have got it right."

"Understood. We shall listen carefully."

As he set out the situation as far as he understood it, Audley tried to relate Sperrhake's disclosures to the interest he might have in any further copy. So far there seemed to have been no question of trade. If anything, Sperrhake had closed the door firmly on any possibility of exchanging bits of paper, and possession of a further copy was not at all essential for his purpose. When he came to the end of his résumé, Audley felt obliged to add a rider to see if he could find some answer to the conundrum.

"I take it therefore that you will not be interested in a second copy as that can hardly affect the value of yours?"

"You are quite right. We are not interested as such in the further copy as you put it. But just as you wish to eliminate all doubts as to the existence of the Fischer copy, we wish to eliminate all doubts as to the existence of the original file which it is suggested contained the official copy. Like you in regard to the letter, we know what is in the file but it is its possession and location that is important. We have the microfilm but we have no proof positive that the original was destroyed. It may be that if there is a further copy of the letter then its present owner may be able to shed light on the fate of the original file. As you see, therefore, we have precisely the same objectives as yourself so that whilst we can give you assurance on the letter, hopefully you can do the same with regard to the file."

Again the proposition was eminently clear. Audley nodded his understanding.

"For that I shall need to get authority. If it is acceptable to you, Herr Sperrhake, I would like to return to London as soon as possible. As you will appreciate, the matter has to be handled very delicately indeed. May I suggest that your organisation should contact me in about ten days or as soon thereafter as is convenient to you, by which time I shall have fresh instructions."

Sperrhake stood up. "Certainly. As Herr Spuhler suggested, however, whilst time is of the essence, we are not bound by any particular timing. I have arranged for the company helicopter to fly you back to Frankfurt, which will then give you the choice of several flights back to London. It's been very pleasant meeting with you and I hope we can conclude our business together to our mutual satisfaction in the near future."

The phraseology was routine. Sperrhake had reverted to type, that of a successful business executive whose word was command. Audley shook hands with both the Germans, intrigued by the continued silence of the older man. He realised that it would be extremely unlikely to find Spuhler volunteering any information so he confined himself to an attempt to memorise the stranger's features on the assumption that he was a man of some importance and therefore could be met again in quite different surroundings and circumstances.

Audley left the hunting lodge with a considerable feeling of relief. Not only had he achieved his objective as far as he possibly could, but his burden was considerably lightened by the thought that he would not be exposed to the twin dangers of Spuhler's driving and the Luftwaffe's flying.

CHAPTER XVII

Accidental Meetings

THERE had been no difficulty in reporting to Clerkenwell. The natural omission had been any reference to a U.K. organisation other than Military Intelligence. Clerkenwell had listened with his usual attentive expression, the only difference in attitude being a change of mannerism from stroking his beard to pulling his ear. He had expressed considerable satisfaction at Audley's achievement and concluded by suggesting that they should both sleep on the matter before deciding what final response should be made to Sperrhake.

Audley returned to his routine without any effort at all. Whether he was on someone's list or not, he certainly would never be missed. His problem was not simple. He had no way of directly approaching his ultimate master, and it wasn't until he was glancing through the sports pages of a *Telegraph* that he suddenly realised that Burleigh was under way. Perhaps that event also enjoyed a Victorian Shadowgraph Tent. Although it would not provide him with any possibility of the contact he sought, he just might renew the acquaintance of the young lady whose work adorned his mantlepiece.

Since, however, he had no wish to waste the best part of the day on a fruitless journey, he telephoned the organisers of the event that evening to enquire whether such a facility was on offer. To his great disappointment, the answer was in the negative. They had no such tent and it required a fairly detailed explanation in order to confirm that fact. His reference to Badminton was not appreciated and in fact brought the conversation to a premature end.

A few days later, Audley was trying to resolve quite a difficult problem. He had a maiden aunt who had certain eccentric characteristics which reminded him of a film version of Miss Marple. She had from time to time descended upon him at school and insisted upon treating him and his cronies at the tuck shop regardless of the consequences. On one occasion, the whole of the school's under-fifteen cricket team was rendered hors de combat by a mountain of sticky cream buns that had disappeared like a mound of honey attacked by a swarm of locusts. For once, the sun had shone. Incredibly the air quivered in the heat and the boys quailed in the advanced stages of satiated appetites. The mixture of rich food and gaseous drink was unrestrainable. The only question that arose was whether the defeat was accelerated by incompetence or an overwhelming desire to retire as quickly as possible to the pavilion.

However, Audley could hardly blame his aunt for that, although he had heard his betters accuse her of killing by kindness. With hindsight he realised that she meant well and she deserved to be remembered accordingly.

The following day was her birthday. Despite her predilection for food normally enjoyed by little boys, she still had excellent taste when it came to presents. Audley had therefore taken a couple of hours off to visit his favourite emporium in Bond Street. He never ceased to be amazed at the glittering glass and silverware on display in Asprey's. At any time of the year it gave the impression of an Aladdin's cave staffed by deferential male assistants and loquacious débutantes. An ideal place in which to pose the question, "What shall I buy for my aunt who has good taste and likes something a little unusual?"

The professionalism of those who helped and advised was of such a standard that the response was never "How much?" One glance at the questioner was all that was needed. Thereafter, a series of objects were presented with loving care and explanation and a final selection conceded. The crowning achievement was the wrapping of the purchase as the physical confirmation that it had been made at Asprey's. Without question it added 10% to the value even though the price was already well inflated.

Audley was half way through this annual ritual when he became aware of a young lady standing alongside him. She was examining him intently. As he turned towards her she suddenly exclaimed: "Yes! I would recognise that nose anywhere. We met at Badminton." Audley was astounded. There standing beside him the very young lady about whom he had been enquiring indirectly a few days before. He had always realised that life was full of coincidences but it would be difficult to imagine one more strange.

"How nice to see you again." His voice was genuine. She looked at him a little quizzically.

"I must admit I did not expect to see you again. You are obviously a town person and I seldom come to London, or indeed any other city if I can possibly help it. As you will have gathered, I am a country person."

Audley glanced down. She was not wearing jodhpurs. In fact, her trim figure was immaculately contained in a quite expensive dress and coat. He decided against any facetious comment.

"You wouldn't by any chance be free for lunch?"

"As a matter of fact I am. The only problem is I haven't got much time. I have to catch the 2.15 p.m. back to Windsor."

Audley mentally noted "Windsor". "Well, I've almost finished here, in fact I have." He turned to the assistant: "Yes, I'll take that little snuff box. It should do very well. I will collect it later on today when you have packed it."

He turned back to the girl. "Have you completed what you intend to do in this establishment? Or have you to be persuaded?"

"I am really looking for ideas," she said. "My father's birthday is next week and he is always very difficult."

"I know what you mean. However, in order to save time perhaps we could go for an early lunch and I could give you some ideas – for your father's present of course – which might be equally helpful?"

She nodded. "Okay. Where shall we go?"

"I would suggest Brown's. If we go out of the rear exit of the shop it's just down Albermarle Street, and not bad at all."

Lunch proved a delightful experience for both; so much so, that Audley suddenly realised that his companion was about to miss her train. "Please let me run you to the station. I have kept you to the point that unless we move, I'm afraid you are going to miss it."

She looked at her watch. "Oh Lord. Daddy's meeting me at the station and he'll be awfully annoyed if I do miss it."

Without more ado, Audley thrust a bundle of notes into the waiter's hand saying, "You can let me have the change later on when I drop in" and, completely out of character, pre-empted a nice old lady who was about to step into a cab. "I'm sure you will not mind madam, but this is an emergency." He jumped into the cab, pulling the young lady with him and leant across her to shut the door. "Paddington, I assume," and repeated it for the benefit of the driver.

As he settled himself in the corner, it suddenly occurred to Audley that he had no idea what the girl's name was. He had enjoyed her company so much he had completely overlooked the possibility of its repetition. "By the way, I've no idea what your name is. Can I ask?"

"My name is Sarah. What's yours?"

The cab took violent action as it endeavoured to circumnavigate Berkeley Square. Conversation was therefore somewhat stilted.

"Audley."

The rest of the journey was relatively uneventful, so much so that they arrived with five minutes to spare at Paddington.

"Have you got a ticket?"

"Yes, thank you."

The two ran across the station, Sarah leading the way armed with the knowledge of the appropriate platform number. As they neared the train it became obvious that they still had a few minutes in hand so they reverted to a more sedate pace.

"Ah, there's Daddy, we have just got time to introduce you." She accelerated and Audley was forced to follow suit. The tall figure who had also caught sight of him looked vaguely familiar. As they approached, he realised to his horror that the eyes fixed on his were those that had drilled him at Badminton. He was about to be introduced to his former control.

"Daddy, this is Audley. He was one of my customers at Badminton and we have just had lunch together at Brown's."

"Pleased to meet you." As he extended his hand, 'Daddy' smiled with his mouth. Fortunately for the two men, Sarah was looking at Audley, and missed what would have otherwise been abundantly clear to her.

"How kind of you to take my daughter to lunch. I am sorry we have to dash but the train is due to leave at any moment now and I have a particular reason for not missing it. So nice to have met you. Come along, dear."

Since the guard was indicating that those who wished to travel by that particular train had better establish their presence on it, the rush of words was consistent with the situation. Sarah waved goodbye to Audley before she disappeared into the commuter train.

Her father turned back to Audley, "We have a problem." Audley nodded. There was nothing he could say. He stood there glumly as the train left the platform. Not for one moment did he expect Sarah's head to appear, in truth he expected never to see her again. The probability made him recall the comments made at his first meeting at the Carlton. He turned on his heel and walked slowly back towards the taxi rank. He doubted whether he could be relieved of his responsibilities, even though his assignment was virtually complete. It was far too late in the day to regret his enthusiastic agreement to the commitment he had undertaken.

The following day the 'phone call was not unexpected. "We must have a talk. Can you meet me tomorrow evening at the Eccentric. I understand you are a member."

"Yes, what time?"

"I would suggest about 7 o'clock."

"Right."

The conversation was extremely brief and without the slightest emotion on either side. Audley felt it did not auger well for their relationship.

The Eccentric has certain advantages. It is very quietly placed in St James, and for those who enjoy a game of snooker it is very well equipped. The only obvious signs of eccentricity are clocks that appear to go backwards and an occasional owl, the explanation for which is often confused and confusing. Audley had become a member initially through his membership of a provincial club, and it seemed an economic way of having an alternative pied-à-terre in town.

The lounge was, as usual, empty. That is of human beings. There was the usual abundance of leather furniture and a couple of hovering stewards. Audley ordered a malt and began to prepare himself for a difficult discussion.

The tall figure entered the lounge precisely on the allotted hour. It seated itself opposite Audley and accepted the invitation offered. After the second malt had been delivered, both men sat in silence having placed their respective drinks on the appropriate side tables. Audley's guest started to drum his fingers on the arm of his chair.

"We have broken the first rule of one-way communication and identification. Except upon installation, we all keep our eyes looking downwards so that we only see those below us. In that way we are no danger to ourselves or to others. We only know that which we are told and we only pass on that which we need to. Had the assignment been less important, I would have cut it short and broken our link. As it is, however, it has to be completed and its significance outweighs even this present problem.

"We must take advantage of the dfificulty. So I would like you to tell me everything that happened during your visit to and from

Selb. You will leave out no detail, however insignificant you think it is."

Audley relaxed. Perhaps they could turn the unacceptable confrontation to advantage. He proceeded to recount his experience, conversations and impressions. He could not have asked for a more attentive listener. When he had concluded, the only confirmation that he received that his report had, indeed, been comprehensive was the absence of questions. The problem had resolved itself into the query "where do we go from here?" After what seemed to Audley to be an interminable silence, his guest gave voice to his decision.

"Once they have it, they have it. There is no point in us seeking to acquire it because even if we were successful they will undoubtedly have made a copy as an insurance. The significance of the letter remains. Its contents are relatively unimportant until they are disclosed supported by the letter itself. It is now simply a question of timing.

"As far as you are concerned, there is nothing further you can do without specific instructions. I think it is extremely unlikely that you will be approached again in this matter. Whether you continue to work for Clerkenwell will be a matter for him to decide, and is of no direct interest to us although obviously circumstances may change. I hope you may have gained something from the experience. There is no need for me to refer to matters of security, confidentiality, etc., I know that we can rely upon your absolute discretion."

The older man slowly extricated himself from the deep, leather armchair. The constant application of various weights and profiles of posteriors had reduced the height of the seat to half that which it was when originally made. The effort required was quite considerable.

Much to Audley's surprise, as he climbed to his feet, he discovered a hand thrust towards him. The handshake conveyed a stronger sense of finality than any exchange of words.

In a matter of seconds, Audley found himself to be the only occupant of the lounge. His glass was empty and, almost without thinking, he flicked the crystal with the nail of his forefinger. Had he given it previous thought, he would not have been surprised at the clear sound that reverberated. As he reseated himself with some embarrassment, the senior steward appeared in the doorway. With some deliberation, he adopted the time-honoured posture of a butler.

"You rang, sir?"

Audley entered into the spirit. "Yes, Jeeves, another malt if you please and some cucumber sandwiches." The butler/steward raised his eyebrows.

"For ready money, sir?"

CHAPTER XVIII

The First Elimination

MORE from curiosity than need, Audley had contacted the Swiss bank which he had been advised at the beginning of his association with Military Intelligence would be the depository for his reward. He had confirmation that that part of the bargain had been consumated.

He had no reason to trust Clerkenwell absolutely and there was always the possibility that knowledge of the arrangement could be as it were, used against him. In the circumstances, therefore, Audley came to the conclusion that he should withdraw the funds and deposit them elsewhere. With that in mind he arranged to fly to Geneva and take advantage of the necessity by staying over night, tasting some of the delights on offer.

The journey from airport to the centre of the city is best accomplished in the bus provided. The cost is a mere 5 Swiss francs compared with 25 units of the same currency if the decision is to go by taxi. With typical Swiss precision, the buses leave every twenty minutes and make the journey at least as quickly as any other vehicle with the possible exception of the odd motorcycle.

All the passengers were discarded at the station, which fortunately was a relatively short walk from the bank which was the purpose of Audley's journey. It is probably true that any significant bank in Geneva – and there are many of them – is in walking distance of the city centre.

It was a private bank and its identification was only by address, and that by inference rather than label. Audley felt that the complete absence of any guide could have been embarrassing had it not been for the inevitable logic of the Swiss that every doorway equalled one number albeit odd on one side and even on the other side of the street.

His business was very soon concluded. All that he did was to ask his bank to close his account and open a new one. The older number became useless and the new one was known only to himself and the dark-suited lawyer who represented the financial institution.

He made his way quickly to the Hotel Du Rhone where he had reserved a reasonably comfortable room. He saw no reason for being extravagant even though he was temporarily in funds. It might well be some time before these would be replenished and the longer that took, the better pleased he would be.

One major problem in Geneva is finding somewhere to eat which is both reasonable in price and quality of fare. The Swiss naturally assume that all visitors must be wealthy, particularly those that stay in the banking centres such as Zurich, Geneva and Basel. Prices are adjusted accordingly. Since it was some years since Audley had last visited that city, he decided to take advice from the Head Porter. He was in the process of awaiting his turn to address the oracle when a familiar voice caused him to turn around with considerable alacrity.

"Hello. What a pleasant surprise!" He was being addressed by Wolfgang Pluzes. Audley's mouth was wide open but he could emit no sound.

Pluzes ignored his reaction. "It would be very pleasant if you were free this evening. I know a marvellous little restaurant that serves German food, which I suppose is not surprising from my point of view. I can thoroughly recommend it and I am quite easy whether we have an early night or visit some club, whichever you prefer."

Audley had recovered. "This is indeed a surprise. I must admit I didn't expect to see you" he paused "in Geneva." "It would be very nice if we could spend the evening together. I could imagine we have much to tell each other!"

Whilst that was undoubtedly so, both men confined the conversation to small talk whilst they were eating, and it wasn't until they had arrived at the coffee stage and were sampling the Davistos cigars that Audley gave voice to that which he had been thinking since they had first met in the Hotel Du Rhone. "What the devil happened to you in the TSE?"

"I recognised someone there who recognised me. If I hadn't, as you say, disappeared at my own volition then I am afraid I would have disappeared inadvertently and inevitably. Having once taken myself out of the action, as it were, I felt I couldn't surface again until it was complete."

Audley understood perfectly. "Well, that explains that, but how do you know that it is complete?"

"I observed your meeting with your friend on the Sunday morning. I think you must have seen me by the way you stared in my direction."

"So you were the one with the glasses. To be absolutely honest, I would never have guessed that."

"No reason why you should, particularly as you believed that I was no longer around."

"So you have surfaced again and things are back to their normal abnormality?"

"Only temporarily. The gentleman I recognised and who recognised me is still in Europe. Even when he returns from whence he came, I am not at all sure that I can stay as I was. I may have to climb."

By now Audley was somewhat confused. He did not understand that reference to Europe, and climbing could hardly apply to mountains. But he had his part of the bargain to meet. He therefore explained to Pluzes the events following the night club episode, including the meeting with his control in Berlin. This gave him the opportunity of asking a direct question. "Does your control know that you are still around?"

"No. With the exception of yourself, I should be surprised and quite dismayed if anyone in our trade was aware of my continued existence."

Audley could not fault the logic. "So why expose yourself to me?"

"Curiosity, really. I would like to know why you are dealing with Asprey?"

"So you know him?"

"Yes, very well. And I must admit I am slightly puzzled. How well do you know him?"

'Only from contact with him and then confined to this particular assignment. He seems to be very influential."

Pluzes looked very thoughtful. He obviously expected more but Audley felt constrained and suddenly very wary. After all, Asprey was in the echelon above and outside Clerkenwell's orbit, whereas Pluzes was on a line with himself and apparently only responsible to his control. Somehow Audley felt that Pluzes might have a duality between East and West but his problem was a conflict of duties other than allegiance and duty.

Pluzes sensed that there would be no further explanations forthcoming. "I can recommend an excellent bar in one of the hotels where the young ladies are not only beautiful, they are intelligent."

Audley signalled for the bill. "And why not?" Since there did not appear to be any impediment on either side, Pluzes suggestion was translated into action. Audley arrived back in his hotel room in the early hours of the morning physically quite tired but relaxed. Mentally, however, it was quite a different condition. He could not shake off a foreboding that the assignment which he thought had sailed beyond his horizon was about to erupt and there was no way in which he would escape the consequences.

One of Audley's many indulgences was to travel in the sharp end of the aeroplane. Since British Airways did not provide a first-class service on the continent, he had no alternative but to fly Swiss Air. In truth, the only inconvenience was that it reduced the choice of flights. The advantage was that he could use the first-class lounge in Geneva Aiport which was extremely well endowed with beverages and comfortable chairs. In these circumstances it was not at all surprising that he left boarding the aircraft until the last possible moment. There was one seat vacant in the small first-class cabin and the one next to it was occupied by Charles Asprey. Neither man expressed surprise at their meeting. Asprey had engineered it and Audley's experience of the previous evening had led him to believe that his new existence would be cluttered with such unexpected happenings.

The two exchanged pleasantries. Since Asprey seemed to have no intention to enter into a serious conversation, Audley decided to leave the initiative with his travelling companion.

"Nasty accident this morning."

"Ah," thought Audley, "this must be it." He said aloud: "Oh, yes?"

"Yes, chap squashed by one of those municipal dustcarts. Apparently in the carly hours of the morning and he was returning to his hotel in an inebriated state. By all accounts he wouldn't have felt a thing. He was anaesthetised by alcohol."

Audley was not quite sure what was expected of him, so he remained silent.

"I believe you may have known him. He looked somewhat like

the fellow who disappeared some months ago in Berlin. If it was, then he has disappeared this time for good. Could be mistaken, of course, because identification after what had happened was not particularly easy, and I only caught a glimpse of him as I passed the scene of the accident."

Audley looked directly at Asprey's profile which remained expressionless. "You mean Pluzes?"

"Was that his name? Whoever he was he isn't."

Audley felt sick. On the few occasions he had been with Pluzes, he had found him an excellent companion with whom he had enjoyed an exceptional rapport.

Asprey continued: "I understand that he was on the point of defecting. You should take note. A man cannot serve two masters without eventually incurring the disfavour of one."

The inference was clear. Suddenly Audley had a thought. He had only Asprey's word for it. When he got back to London he would get Clerkenwell to check it out.

Since Asprey had no further information to convey, the conversation ceased. Audley saw no point in maintaining contact. As he was in the aisle seat, he was amongst the first out of the 'plane. There was no sign of Asprey in the baggage collection area and as soon as his own luggage arrived Audley quickly made his way to the car park and from there drove home.

By sheer coincidence Audley had no need to go to Clerkenwell for confirmation. There on the front page of the *Telegraph* was a short report which repeated Asprey's information almost word for word. The only difference was the reporter identified the unfortunate victim as an unnamed German. Print has the finality of an obituary. It is difficult to accept death when the news is conveyed by word of mouth. The mere act of folding the newspaper seemed to put the seal on the fact that this time Audley was quite convinced that he would never see Pluzes again. Curiously enough, despite Asprey's comment on the dangers attached to having two masters, Audley did not feel that there but for the Grace of God. . . . If anything, the confirmation served to re-emphasise that for him the assignment was indeed over. Perhaps it would have been but for a coincidence that no one could possibly have foreseen.

CHAPTER XIX

The Wine Cellars

ALTHOUGH extremely quiet, the voice was immediately recognisable. "Hello, Audley. I wonder if we could meet in the near future?" Audley took a few moments to recollect his thoughts. These had been interrupted by the telephone but continued to dominate his mind.

"Oh, hello Charles. Long time no hear." It was an inane response but at least it gave him time to readjust.

"Yes," Charles sounded somewhat impatient, "and not unnaturally. How about this Saturday?"

Audley was now on the right wavelength. "Yes, that would be all right. When and where?"

"Do you know Bristol?"

"A little. I used to visit Clifton from time to time."

"Good. I suggest we meet at a quiet restaurant called Harveys which is in Denmark Street off the old centre. I will arrange a table and we can meet in the entrance lobby at about 7.30 p.m. We will not be using our own names."

Audley translated that to mean that Asprey would not be using his name for the reservation. "Fine, see you there. Bye." Audley was vaguely aware of Harveys, although the connotation was one of sherry rather than restaurants. Nevertheless, he could remember comment being made during one of his visits to Clifton.

As a matter of fact, although there were many fine restaurants in and around London, they all suffered from the same defect. They were remarkably expensive. Audley, although not mean, liked value for money. The opportunity of dining well in the provinces had certain attractions. Since he had no more than family commitments for the coming week-end, he could see no problem in rearranging his timetable.

The journey from London to Bristol can be accomplished with equal comfort by road or rail provided that if the choice is the former, the departure from Town does not coincide with the rush hour. Audley opted to travel by car on the premise that it would provide him with greater flexibility for his return, which he arranged should be on the Sunday. There was no point in restricting one's capacity to enjoy alcohol in conjunction with excellent food. It was thus quite logical to arrange overnight accommodation at the Grand Hotel, which is aptly located in Broad Street although that is probably the narrowest two-way dead-end thoroughfare in the city.

It was fortunate that the inadequacy of the hotel with regard to its car-parking facilities was compensated by its proximity to Harveys restaurant. That, coupled with a fine evening, provided Audley with the opportunity of a gentle stroll around the centre of the birth-place of merchant venturers, the hotel and restaurant being situated at approximately opposite corners of that lozenge.

The entrance to the restaurant was in a narrow street behind the Hippodrome. The visitor descended into the warm inviting interior that centuries ago provided the cellarage in which the liquid treasures of the city were stored. Coincidentally, the upper structure had been a monastery. Bristol was indeed a city of contrast. It had enjoyed a long commercial life, and the contentment accumulated by the effort and perspiration of others for the sedate satisfaction of the resident pillars of society.

Its wealth has depended upon trade and it is no coincidence that one of its main shopping areas is known as Whiteladies Road and Blackboys Hill. Although local legend has it that manacles still exist in certain cellars which were used as temporary accommodation for black slaves, the bulk of this profitable business was conducted at a comfortable arm's length of some three thousand miles.

Audley had been vaguely aware of a possible relationship between Harveys of Bristol and sherry, but his first visit to the restaurant of that name left him in no doubt as to the connection between the two. The main decorative feature in the entrance lobby leading to the cellars was a wall composed entirely of empty bottles. The white bricks behind the long bar were buttressed by sherry casks supporting the ancient figure-head of a schooner which presumably had transported the golden liquid from the plains of Spain to the mud of the old Bristol city docks.

Although created from the cellars beneath an ancient monastery, the restaurant was in no way claustrophobic. The plush burgundy of the seating was in contrast to the plain décor adopted for walls and ceiling.

Audley was met by Franco, the highly professional and competent restaurant manager, formally dressed as befitted his office.

"Good evening sir, you are with . . ." Before Franco had time to complete his question, he noted the gleam of recognition in Audley's eye and responded accordingly.

"Ah, I see you are with that gentleman over there, you are most welcome." Franco hovered to receive Asprey's instructions which he duly passed on to the barman.

"This is your first visit to this establishment?" asked Asprey.

"Yes, it looks very attractive."

Asprey handed over one of the large menus which were already in his possession. "The choice is quite extensive. The food ain't bad; in fact it's quite good and the servings are substantial. The outstanding feature of this restaurant is its wine list. At one time it was reputed to be the longest in Europe. I doubt that it remains so. Nevertheless, it contains a very fine selection of claret. If you would care to leave the selection of wine to me, I am sure you will find it exceedingly palatable."

Audley was only too relieved to agree. The menu by itself was formidable. He would be more than happy to leave any further decisions to his host.

Asprey obviously had no intention of discussing the purpose of their meeting but since he was remarkably well informed on the history of Bristol in general and its relationship with the wine trade, the time passed very pleasantly. He had managed to arrange table thirteen, which was very discreetly placed in an alcove. Nevertheless, they had completed their main course before he revealed his plans.

"Harveys not only have very extensive cellars in which they keep a very large stock of wine, there is also a unique museum and a reconstruction of a medieval public house. I thought we might kill two birds with one stone – take advantage of the absolute privacy and at the same time extend our own experience."

Audley confirmed that it was an excellent idea. Since he anticipated quite a lengthy session, however, he decided he ought to go to the men's room so that he would be at least physically relaxed. The toilets were near to the entrance and not difficult to find. It was on his return journey through the restaurant that he heard her laugh. He had no doubt that it was Sarah. He decided that he needed to make a detour. He had not been mistaken. Sarah was seated at a table for two tucked behind one of the pillars. Her companion was a young man, casually dressed. He was obviously recounting a tale of great interest. Sarah was sitting with her face cupped in her hands leaning towards him, concentrating on every word. Audley toyed with the idea of interrupting their obvious tête-à-tête but he quickly realised how inappropriate from every point of view that might be. Reluctantly he continued towards table thirteen.

As soon as he had rejoined Asprey, Franco appeared to enquire if they were now ready to visit the musuem and pub. Asprey readily confirmed that they were, so they followed the manager to the far end of the restaurant where he pulled aside a curtain to disclose a door whose existence was clearly defined by a heavy mortice lock.

Once through the door, Franco's first action was to press a number of light switches which made it possible for them to progress into the narrow cellars. The lights were unevenly spaced. Where they were grouped in a cluster a large area of bins and passageways was clearly to be seen. Where they were spread apart, they provided individual shafts of light which emphasised the impenetrable darkness which divided one from the other.

Franco continued to lead the way, pointing out the homes of innumerable alcoholic beverages steeped in history, tradition and cobweb. Whilst it was likely that brandy of 150 years of age and port of one-third of that venerability could still be enjoyed in the way its makers intended, the value of prestigious wines of great age lay ironically more in the homage accorded to the label and the unopened bottle than to the possible satisfaction achieved by drinking its contents.

If beauty is in the eye of the beholder, then value can only be found in the imagination of the fanatic. Franco waxed lyrically and with obvious pride on the qualifications and uniqueness of his prisoners. Audley shivered slightly. There was a very narrow divide between cellars and dungeons. The antiquity of his surroundings had a chill which was more than physical.

"Now may I offer you a glass of our excellent port in the Elizabethan pub?" Obviously they had come to the end of their tour and Franco was now placing at their disposal his pièce de résistance.

"Thank you very much," said Asprey. "I wonder if you could leave us for a little time whilst we savour both the excellent port and this unique atmosphere? I would be very greatly obliged if this could be arranged." He laughed and added: "I can assure you we have no intention of sampling further."

Franco laughed in return. "Certainly. I will leave all the lights on so you will have no problem in finding your way out. There is plenty of time before we close and I will make sure that someone comes for you in case you should overlook the hour."

Asprey, having expressed his thanks, waited until he heard the door open and shut at the far end of the cellars.

"Now to business. I have managed to get hold of the copy letter. In fact I have it with me. I am not going to destroy it, neither am I going to hand it over to you."

Asprey put his hand in his pocket but instead, as Audley had anticipated, of it re-emerging holding an envelope, Audley found himself looking down the barrel of a rather large pistol. Its size was due almost entirely to the silencer which added significantly to its already unpleasant appearance.

"Yes," continued Asprey, "I am afraid we have to part company here. I had thought of drugging you and then pretending you were drunk, but that would only have been deferring the inevitable."

"But why kill me?" asked Audley. "We are both on the same side ultimately. Indeed you are my link."

"Unfortunately, you are wrong on all counts. We are not part of the same organisation. The insidious secrecy in which yours immerses itself has enabled me to trespass with impunity. It is true that my organisation is comparable to yours since we both exist to perpetuate the security of our respective nations. Yet there is a significant difference. When the time is right, we are overt leaders. Even in times of crisis, those who hold the power in your country will never expose themselves further than as members of an inner committee. But above all, your roots are much deeper and wider than ours, entangled with and strangled by your history."

Audley raised his hands slowly as an expression of disbelief. "So, we are on opposite sides but we have similar objectives. Why do wish to kill me?"

"For the simple reason that you know me, that you can recognise me."

"But we may never meet again and to whom should I, as it were, give you away?"

"I am not at all sure that you should not die in ignorance.

However, I will tell you one thing and one thing only. It is my privilege to lead the Fourth Reich."

"So you are German?"

"Of course. I am not sure if I should be flattered or insulted by your inability to recognise my origins. However, it is of no concern now."

Asprey raised the pistol which, despite its length, he held without the slightest waiver. For a split second Audley could not make up his mind whether he should shut his eyes or not.

Both men heard it. Both men disbelieved it. A deprecatory cough inserted itself between them. Asprey cursed and glanced quickly behind him. Audley jumped forward and grabbed his executioner's right hand. Instead of responding, Asprey froze and the two men remained like statues, representing a meeting between two friends who had firmly clasped their hands. The voice was without direction. It came out of the darkness around them.

"May I suggest you disentangle yourselves and Herr Asprey drop your gun, holding it first by its snout, all very deliberately and positively, please." The disembodied instructions were followed to the letter.

"Good. I do not intend to lecture either of you but I must say Mr Lonsdale you are extremely naïve and if I were your employer I would regard you as a liability. On the other hand, I suppose I ought to thank you for encouraging Herr Asprey to be with us tonight."

The soft incisive tone returned. "I am sure you will have guessed my next request, Herr Asprey. Please be good enough to place the envelope on the bar top. I shall assume that you may well have a second weapon on your person and therefore I shall not hesitate to shoot you at any untoward movement. Now please do as I say."

For a split second Asprey hesitated. Then he shrugged his shoulders and pulled an envelope out of his jacket inside pocket. He placed it gently on the bar as directed.

"Thank you. That will do excellently."

The words were terminated by a second cough louder than the first. Asprey was thrown forward and to his horror, Audley saw a fountain of blood spurt from the back of his head.

"Do not move, Mr Lonsdale. It is just possible I may let you live. Not only should you savour the next few moments, but anticipate that they need not be your last."

The voice now sounded very near. Indeed, as Audley strained his eyes in a vain attempt to pierce the gloom around him, he suddenly became aware of a figure emerging into the light. At first he did not recognise him. Then as the murderer's features came into relief, he recalled the name of the man that he had met in East Berlin. "Herr Zeigner! How? Why?"

The German laughed. "I can quite understand your astonishment, Herr Lonsdale. We have been following Herr Asprey ever since he foolishly returned to Europe. We knew because of his connections in Germany that sooner or later he would obtain what we all sought since he or his successor would undoubtedly be a prime negotiator in any reunification operations."

Herr Zeigner picked up the envelope and held it out to Audley. "I am sure your leader would give a King's ransom for the contents, but I shall enjoy an even higher price. If I had time, I would almost certainly give you the opportunity of reading it, but then I would definitely have to kill you. As it is, I only need to render you hors de combat which, if you co-operate, will be temporarily painful but at least you will wake up in this world. Now which is it to be: your co-operation or your termination?"

"I think that's your choice, Herr Zeigner. Please stand still."

For one terrible moment Audley wondered if he were taking part in a second-rate farce. Fortunately for his sanity, he was no longer allowed to remain a spectator.

"Now Mr Lonsdale, please step away from Herr Zeigner – to your left, and then remain perfectly still."

Audley did as he was told.

"Now, like Herr Asprey, you Herr Zeigner must have worked out my next request. Will you please replace the envelope on the bar top. Good."

There was a moment of silence. In that short space of time, Audley sensed more than one presence hidden from the glare of lights above the medieval public house. He obtained his confirmation from the next set of instructions.

"Having done that, we are willing to let you go back to your masters, Herr Zeigner. You will walk steadily and discreetly out of these cellars and the restaurant and you will return to Moscow as quickly as possible. You will not contact anyone in this country. You will find a seat reserved for you on the first flight from Heathrow, which you should be able to catch quite comfortably. We will have you under observation the whole time, and I can assure you that any attempt to take advantage of my generosity and we will mete out the same treatment that you gave to our friend over there. Do you understand and do you agree?"

"Yes, on both counts. May I now move?"

"Yes, but be careful."

Herr Zeigner looked quizzically at Audley and then calmly set off to do precisely that which he had been instructed. His footsteps echoed through the cellars, their repetition ceasing when the door opened and closed. The silence was broken by a slight scuffle of feet and then the question was asked: "Has he definitely gone?"

"Yes."

Audley started at the affirmative. It had been given by a female, and the voice was again that of Sarah's.

To complete his confusion, the young man who then stepped into the light had been her companion in the restaurant earlier that evening. The newcomer appreciated Audley's reaction and waved his hand generally in his direction. "Now is not the time for explanations. We have one or two loose ends to tie up here. I suggest you return to your hotel. We will settle the bill. At 11 o'clock tomorrow morning you will be at the Bear at Hungerford – I assume you know where that is." There was no pause for confirmation. "You will stay in your car in the car park. Now, I would be grateful if you would leave straight away."

The young man had picked up the envelope from the bar top and stuffed it into his pocket. Audley thought seriously for one moment of attempting to speak with Sarah but quickly realised that it would be an utter waste of time and effort. It wasn't until he walked through the door into the restaurant that he realised how cold the cellars really were. Most of the customers had already left and no one appeared to take the slightest interest in his progress towards the exit.

Despite his original belief to the contrary. Audley did in fact sleep rather well, so much so that he had little time to spare to make his intended 'phone call before he had to check out. As it was, he arrived at the Bear with just three minutes in hand, thankful that it was a Sunday morning and the traffic had been reasonable.

At 11 o'clock precisely a black Range Rover pulled alongside his vehicle. Its driver leaned across and beckoned towards Audley. His intentions were quite clear. Audley was being invited to join him. It was not an invitation to be ignored.

CHAPTER XX

The Queen of the Cotswolds Survives

THE Range Rover was an ideal vehicle in which to traverse the countryside. Its driver had the advantage of an elevated position in order to see traffic in advance of confrontation on the acute bends. The passengers could enjoy the scenery from their position of vantage. Finally, should a detour be required in order to avoid a tractor or a lumbering herd of cattle, the four-wheeled drive transformed fields of grass, and indeed mud, into acceptable alternatives to metalled lanes.

It was indeed a glorious day and Audley did his best to enjoy it.

They had long since left the main road and had passed through several villages when they turned between two massive stone pillars that obviously guarded the approach to a large estate. A substantial Cotswold stone house, the result of expanding the original lodge, was the object of their journey. The Range Rover passed its main entrance and parked discreetly amongst the outbuildings at the rear of the property.

The driver, who had not spoken a word, switched off his engine and again entirely by signal indicated to Audley that he should enter the house. This was easily achieved as the heavy oaken door was already open. Standing just inside was a bearded figure, dressed in country tweed, the very model of a game-keeper. That he was not became immediately apparent when he addressed Audley.

"Lovely morning. You must have had a very pleasant run from Hungerford." He obviously had no intention of waiting for a reply. "If you will follow me to the study?"

Fortunately, his guide was of equal height, so that Audley had ample warning of the need to duck almost continuously as they passed under blackened beams that seemed to insert themselves in the ceilings without rhyme or reason. It had often occurred to Audley that either people generally were of considerably shorter stature some three hundred years previously or they must have enjoyed the challenge he had seen written in similar buildings and on similar beams 'to duck or grouse'.

The habit had become so repetitive that when his guide opened the final double doors with the announcement "This is the study" he passed between them in a quite unnecessary semi-crouch. His control was standing in the centre of a long and rather narrow room, the contents of which resembled an antique shop rather than a domestic domain.

"Thank you for coming. I realise that you had little alternative, but in view of the unexpected developments last night I felt the least I could do was to offer you a full explanation. Now, if you will bear with me I will endeavour to put those events into context so that hopefully you will leave here somewhat less confused than you are at the present time."

"I must admit," said Audley, "there are one or two bits of the jigsaw which don't fit as far as I can see, and there are one or two gaps as well."

The taller man waved his hand towards the corner seat. He was obviously in a hurry to convey his thoughts and had little time for comments which added nothing to the comprehension. "If we sit down over there then we shall be reasonably comfortable."

The corner of the room was in fact a continuous leaded window and its seat commanded a very pleasant view of the gardens. It was well cushioned and both men visibly relaxed.

The older man paused to collect his thoughts, before embarking upon his explanation.

"When two nations declare war against each other and agree that a state of hostility exists, it is generally assumed that all communication between them ceases forthwith. This is not so. Whilst it is true that the main arteries are severed and then securely cauterised, there is still a complex web of veins and vessels which, certainly in the case of Europe, has grown and developed over many centuries, regardless of changes in national boundaries and economic advantages.

"The methods of communication employed range from face-to-face conversation, such as took place in neutral locations like Lisbon and Stockholm during the 1939–45 War, transmission of documents in neutral diplomatic pouches, to business connections that continue to thrive despite the efforts of the opponents.

"The popular image of a spy tapping out a message in morse hidden in the loft of some remote farmhouse in occupied territory is but one example – albeit one requiring great courage – of the need for information without which a war may be won and lost.

"There is no doubt that during conflict Military Intelligence is a necessity. Therefore its gathering is depicted as a heroic task at least equal to the contribution of those who risk their lives on the field of battle. This façade of glamour to encourage enlistment clouds the basic need of any nation to be continuously aware of the intentions of its neighbours and those facts that it should know in determining its own strategy. So in times of so-called peace, as the glamour recedes and the urgency of military conflict is no longer the excuse or the reason, politicians introduce the crumbling front of national security as a means of continuing the gathering of information that could be related to war-like activity and pursuits. Intelligence is always a necessity. Its constituent elements are determined by the national strategy. If that is economic power, as may be the objcctive of Japan and Germany, then the strategic information that is required will differ considerably from that which is sought where the target is political domination.

"In this country particularly, and to a certain extent in Germany also, we have enjoyed the advantage that for centuries our society has enabled us to operate an interrelated system of Intelligence through two sources of power; namely, those intent on political domination and those determined upon national survival whatever the colour of Parliament. The demarcation between the two is relatively clear in times of peace, but where the short-term expediency of winning a war exists, there is much closer liaison.

"Unfortunately, our view of history is governed more by propaganda than objective analysis. Quite often, events within this country are presented with greater integrity by those outside it, who as observers enjoy the privilege of a wider canvas. Even so, those who advised Hitler, always assuming that he listened to them, on the structure of our sources of power and the hierarchy of our society in the 1940s made a basic error. They concluded that the Establishment and the aristocracy were positioned as they had been in the nineteenth century. They were wrong. Hence our present predicament.

"It is true that the ambitions of the House of Saxe-Coburg were limitless within Europe and that this family permeated most capitals. It is also correct that its field control – to use our modern terminology – was one Baron Christian Stockmar, whose influence even in this country was enormous. But the creation of a European kingdom was simply never on. It's difficult enough to get agreement within a family living in one house, but to expect near and distant relatives in terms of both blood and location to work together for a common goal was to hope for the impossible. Victoria and Albert did their utmost, and I have no doubt that at one stage it must have seemed that they had achieved the impossible, but Albert's death and Victoria's withdrawal from society opened the gates of personal ambition, greed and envy. The First World War was inevitable. I would commend Sir Richard Attenborough's direction of 'Oh, what a luverly war!' as an insight into the reasons for and the conduct of that terrible tragic farce. Nevertheless, whatever else it might have lost, it did provide the rock upon which the house of Saxe-Coburg and all its ambitions ultimately foundered.

"But to return to our main theme. There was a chasm between the English aristocracy and those who despite their station were regarded as foreigners and for a number of years the latter held the overt reigns of power. But that chasm has long since been bridged and their respective descendents, although probably retaining some distance, are no longer at odds with each other. And it would appear that it was that development that Hitler had overlooked.

"Hence his letter based upon the presumption that there would be common ground. He tapped the wrong vein. We knew it was coming, so we intercepted it.

"The mere fact that the Führer had sued for peace was not and is not particularly embarrassing. It had been widely recognised that certain factions in English society had more than passing admiration for his achievements. One could go one stage further and suggest that even the naming of names could have been absorbed and glossed over. There had to be something more, much more, to support the efforts made first to destroy it and later to incarcerate its courier.

"So let us consider a hypothetical possibility. Suppose that some persons in this country were privy to Operation Barbarossa, the invasion of the U.S.S.R. Suppose that the only critical fact not known was the intended date of attack. Assume that Hess was close to Hitler, that during the years 1939, 1940 and 1941 he had been involved in the planning of Operation Barbarossa. Would he have known the probable date of invasion in May 1941 as being, as indeed it was, June 1941? Would he have declared that under intensive interrogation, yet it was not reported? If Hitler was seeking the neutrality of the United Kingdom, could the quid pro quo have been the inactivity of neutrality for the avoidance of destruction? The benefit to us must have seemed remarkably clear to the Führer, since it was only a matter of time before he would destroy us utterly. The attractions to Germany of Britain's neutrality during the attack on Russia were equally significant. The British Navy would not be able to protect the convoys essential for Russia's continuance in the battle. The British could not act as a staging post for supplies. There could be no offer of British technological help – radar, training and, perhaps, even nuclear developments. It would appear quite reasonable to suppose that a deal could be made.

"The Russians already distrusted the British. They had since at least 1812, when they deliberately restrained themselves from destroying Napoleon, as they could easily have done, in order to prevent the British from entering France unopposed and thus the opportunity of following in French footsteps to the gate of Moscow. If they could resist the temptation to destroy their greatest enemy of the time, then their fear of this country must surely have been great. And so it has persisted; and who is to know what our reaction to Hitler might have been had he actually succeeded in his intent to conquer the Soviets?

"So the publication of any suggestion of such negotiations would have affected our relations with Stalin and his successors for many many years. Even if it became clear that we had not responded to Hitler's overtures, suppose evidence suggested that we knew of Operation Barbarossa in such detail that our silence on it could be interpreted as being, shall we say, unfriendly towards our allies?

"But these are all suppositions, and without this letter must remain as such. And there is one further salient feature. From all published records, it would appear that Churchill had been satisfied with the superficial story, and confused the official version by introducing a comparison with his own assistant that involved the use of a captured British Spitfire, although it was quite illogical in the context used. Nevertheless, it gave credence to the theory that Hess had used a Spitfire and therefore was alone. At a later date, when victory was in sight, Stalin indirectly suggested that even the British Prime Minister did not always know the whole story.

"The original has been destroyed. We have the first copy. There is no point in destroying that as clearly another must now exist, probably in Bavaria. Those who hold that will expose it when it suits their purpose. Which brings me to Asprey. He was, as you now know, a founder member of the Fourth Reich and a potential negotiator in the reunification of Germany. He is no longer with us, but I doubt whether he will be missed. The plans of which he was an essential part have had to be delayed so that his eventual role would have passed to someone else, anyway. His loss is our gain, as he was one of the very few who understood how the British Navy were on the right spot at the right time to sink U124, and also had a shrewd idea as to its contents. He could have put his knowledge to considerable use and our discomfort. In his absence we may be able to use the time left to us to de-fuse the bomb before it is set off. Now I will pause at this point to give you the opportunity of asking any questions you may have and also to seek some small refreshment."

Audley's instructor levered himself from his comfortable arm-chair and moved across to a side-board. "Would you care to join me?"

Audley responded: "Thank you very much, a small whisky and a large soda if you please." The older man poured identical drinks. Audley asked the first question that came to mind. "What is the role of the K.G.B. in this?"

"Ah, yes, our friend Zeigner. Nasty chap, but very thorough and professional. Pity we had to let him go, but on balance the best option. The K.G.B. have literally been dying to put their hands on the letter ever since they became aware of the existence of the copy. I fear Frau Fischer has taken the same route. They may even oppose reunification of the two Germany's in order to persuade the present owners to part with it, but that's unlikely at this stage. If they had it in their possession they would not only greatly embarrass the British Government by the consequential revelations then evidenced, but they would be able to identify that echelon of British Intelligence that Blunt and his mob tried to infiltrate and failed. Those particular traitors attempted to straddle the divide between the professional organisation responsible to the P.M. and the hierarchy which we represent and is responsible only to itself. To be fair, they nearly succeeded, not through their ability but because of our complacency. A lesson hopefully well learnt. Finally, they could eradicate the names of their agents set out in the letter."

"So the K.G.B. will try again?"

"Without the slightest doubt, but most likely through the East German route and again looking for an aide in the German hierarchy rather than its Military Intelligence."

"The other question," continued Audley: "I can understand the embarrassment and the mistrust, etc., but why go to the extreme of keeping Churchill in the dark, if he ever was?"

His control looked at his watch. "Just as well you only have two questions. I must away very shortly. Since you ask, and I think you are entitled to know, I will tell you. The letter carried by Hess was a reply. Consider the implications of that. Who wrote the previous letter? For what purpose? How long had there been correspondence? Between whom? Does that answer your question?"

Audley nodded. He could think of nothing to say.

"Now, if you will excuse me. John will run you back to Hungerford. You should be comfortably back in Town for tea. Same arrangements as before. I will contact you when you are needed. Until then, keep Clerkenwell happy and try to return to normality. It may be quite a while before you will hear from me, so make the most of it."

The two men shook hands. John appeared as if by magic and led Audley out into the yard at the rear of the house where the Range Rover patiently waited. Almost simultaneously, a dark green Bentley Mulsanne swept up the front drive and slid to a gravel-crunching stop. Its driver, a grey man in a grey suit made his way without announcement into the study to deliver his report.

"Everything according to instructions. The device is timed to action thirty minutes after activation and that will occur when the engine is switched on. The car's in excellent condition, so with reasonable luck no one else will be involved." For a moment it seemed as though he was about to salute. Instead he stood with his eyes fixed on his commander.

"Well done. It's a pity, but we have no alternative. Nice chap, but much too naïve and knows too much. Still, a pity." The tall, thin frame stooped just for a second. Then the shoulders pushed back, the hands were placed in the small of the back and the incisiveness returned. "That's all. Come back in about an hour's time. We have to go back to the house. You can have a bite to eat in the kitchen here while you wait."

The chauffeur left as quickly as he had arrived. His master settled himself at his desk and began dictating a report. The hour had almost passed when the study door opened and a head of curly brown hair thrust itself around the jamb.

"I say, Father, are you ready?"

"Yes, just coming. You can enter. I've just finished."

"Good." The young man whose hair was the envy of many a young lady was of the same build as his parent. His dress was immaculate, almost to the state of foppishness, yet he did not give the impression of being a young buck. His speech was incisive, quick and clear. Obviously, he knew what he wanted from life and had not the slightest doubt but that it would be achieved. His experience to date confirmed his aspirations.

His father was bending over a drawer into which he was returning his machine. His voice appeared to come from a distance. "By the way, is Sarah coming with us?"

"No, s'matter of fact she's not. Seems she has a date."

"Oh, yes. Who with?"

"Don't know, but I think you've met him quite recently."

The parent slowly straightened his back. The next question was asked very deliberately and quietly. "Any idea where she was meeting her friend and when?"

"Yes, they were meeting at the Bear at Hungerford where she intended to leave her car, as they were then going to visit her favourite village in the Cotswolds. You know, the one she's for ever going on about. It's near a place called Paradise, with a beacon from which Cromwell lobbed a cannon ball into Gloucester, and all that kind of stuff. Apparently, our ancestors had some connection there. Something to do with the church. Whether they intend to take evening service, I know not. But in any event, he has to be back in Town before cock-crow, so she won't be home that late."

His father looked at his watch. The journey to Hungerford took the Range Rover some twenty minutes. That time had long since elapsed, but they might have stopped at the Bear for a drink or even a snack. He waved his hand at his son. "Would you mind going ahead in your own car? I've just got to make a phone call and it may take a few minutes. Don't want to keep your mother waiting for both of us."

His son started towards the door, sensing something amiss. "No, not at all. In fact, it will suit me better as I was going to the Park this afternoon for the polo. See you later."

There was no reply. His father was rapidly turning over the pages of a telephone directory. His search was short and the connection almost immediate. The request was simple.

"I wonder if you would page a Mr Lonsdale, who I believe may be with you either in the bar or in the restaurant. It is extremely urgent. Yes, I will wait."

As he acknowledged the response, he lowered himself slowly into the chair behind his desk. The knuckles of his left hand which gripped the receiver were white with fiery red spots. His eyes were without focus, fixed unseeingly on infinity. He already knew the answer. Who would waste time in a dusty pub when the rolling green hills of England beckoned and the shy sun had for once decided to add its blessing to that glorious countryside? When all the world loved a lover and lovers loved the world? For some inexplicable reason, a painfully learnt and jealously retained sonnet thrust itself into his mind.

"Oh, mistress mine, where art thou roaming. Oh stay and hear your true love's coming, that can sing both high and low. Trip no further, pretty sweeting, journies end in lovers' meetings, That every wise man's son doth know. What is love?" The words flowing through his mind were interrupted by the voice in his ear. Its message was short and as expected.

His automatic "Thank you" was mumbled into space, as he replaced the receiver without releasing his grip. He had not cried since the first night in the dormitory of his prep-school.